PENGUIN
VITAE

WHAT CLASSIC BOOKS would you place together on a shelf to represent the course of your life? This is the question that sparks our hardcover series Penguin Vitae, or loosely translated, "Penguin of one's life." A diverse world of storytellers from the past speak to us at pivotal chapters of our lives and connect a community of readers across time and generations. Penguin Vitae invites readers to curate their own personal Penguin Classics canon from this series and to discover other seminal works of timeless inspiration, intellectual engagement, and creative originality. To enrich the reader's experience of these gift editions, Paul Buckley designs bold, typographic covers inspired by each work, with vibrant foil stamping and colored endpapers, contributing to Penguin's acclaimed history of innovative book design.

We hope you find yourself within Penguin Vitae, discover something new, and share these classic books with others.

ELDA ROTOR
Publisher
Penguin Classics

Clare Kendry is living on the edge. Light-skinned, elegant, and ambitious, she is married to a racist white man unaware of her African American heritage, and has severed all ties to her past after deciding to "pass" as a white woman. Clare's childhood friend, Irene Redfield, just as light-skinned, has chosen to remain within the African American community, and is simultaneously allured and repelled by Clare's risky decision to engage in racial masquerade for personal and societal gain. After frequenting African American–centric gatherings together in Harlem, Clare's interest in Irene turns into a homoerotic longing for Irene's black identity that she abandoned and can never embrace again, and she is forced to grapple with her decision to pass for white in a way that is both tragic and telling. This edition features a new introduction by Emily Bernard and notes by Thadious M. Davis.

PENGUIN CLASSICS

PASSING

NELLA LARSEN, one of the most acclaimed and influential writers of the Harlem Renaissance, was born Nellie Walker on April 13, 1891, in Chicago. In the 1910s she came to New York, where she worked as a nurse and a librarian, and in 1919 she married a research physicist. She began publishing stories in the mid-1920s and published her first novel, *Quicksand*, in 1928. *Passing* came out the following year. Larsen was awarded a William E. Harmon Bronze Award for Distinguished Achievement Among Negroes and a Guggenheim fellowship. Encountering personal and professional struggles, she was unable to have her third novel accepted for publication and by the end of the 1930s had stopped writing altogether. She worked full time as a nurse until her death in 1964.

EMILY BERNARD is the author of *Carl Van Vechten and the Harlem Renaissance: A Portrait in Black and White*. Her other books include *Remember Me to Harlem: The Letters of Langston Hughes and Carl Van Vechten* (2001), which was a *New York Times* Notable Book of the Year; *Some of My Best Friends: Writers on Interracial Friendships* (2004), chosen by the New York Public Library as a Book for the Teen Age; and *Michelle Obama: The First Lady in Photographs* (2009), a book she coauthored with Deborah Willis, which received a 2010 NAACP Image Award. Her essays have been published in several anthologies and journals, such as *The American Scholar, Oxford American* magazine, *The Best American Essays, Best African American Essays*, and *The Best Creative Nonfiction*. She is a professor of English and Critical Race and Ethnic Studies at the University of Vermont.

THADIOUS M. DAVIS is Geraldine R. Segal Professor of American Social Thought and Professor of English at the University of Pennsylvania and the author of *Nella Larsen: Novelist of the Harlem Renaissance*. She previously taught at Vanderbilt University, Brown University, and the University of North Carolina at Chapel Hill. She has been a fellow at the Newberry Library in Chicago, the Huntington Library in San Marino, California, and the Center for Scholars and Writers at the New York Public Library. She is the editor of the Penguin Classics edition of Nella Larsen's *Quicksand*.

NELLA LARSEN

PASSING

**INTRODUCTION AND
SUGGESTIONS FOR FURTHER READING BY**
Emily Bernard

NOTES BY
Thadious M. Davis

PENGUIN BOOKS

PENGUIN BOOKS

An imprint of Penguin Random House LLC
penguinrandomhouse.com

First published in the United States of America by Alfred A. Knopf Inc., 1929
Edition with an introduction and notes by Thadious M. Davis published in Penguin Books 1997
Previous edition with an introduction by Emily Bernard published in Penguin Books 2018
This edition published 2020

ISBN 9780143129424 (hardcover)

LIBRARY OF CONGRESS CATALOGING-IN-PUBLICATION DATA
Names: Larsen, Nella, author. | Bernard, Emily, 1967–
Title: Passing / Nella Larsen ; introduction and suggestions for
further reading by Emily Bernard ; notes by Thadious M. Davis.
Description: New York, New York : Penguin Books, 2018.
Identifiers: LCCN 2017035808 (print) | LCCN 2017040181 (ebook) |
ISBN 9781101191156 (ebook) | ISBN 9780142437278 (paperback)
Subjects: LCSH: African American women—Fiction. | Racially mixed people—Fiction. |
Identity (Psychology)—Fiction. | Passing (Identity)—Fiction. | Female friendship—Fiction. |
Human skin color—Fiction. | New York (N.Y.)—Fiction. |
Married women—Fiction. | Psychological fiction.
Classification: LCC PS3523.A7225 (ebook) | LCC PS3523.A7225 P37 2018 (print) |
DDC 813/.54—dc23
LC record available at https://lccn.loc.gov/2017035808

Printed in the United States of America
1   3   5   7   9   10   8   6   4   2

CONTENTS

PASSING

INTRODUCTION

Got on the train
Didn't have no fare,
But I rode some,
I rode some.
> —Zora Neale Hurston,
> "Mule Bone"

Passing is a work of fiction, but it is a true story about the world in which its author, Nella Larsen, lived. To describe it simply as a novel about a black woman passing for white would be to ignore the multiple layers of its concerns. *Passing* is about the monumental cultural transformations that took place in American society after World War I. It is about changing definitions of concepts like race and gender, and the inextricable relationship between whiteness and blackness. It is a meditation on the uneasy dynamic between social obligation and personal freedom. It dramatizes the impossibility of self-invention in a society in which nuance and ambiguity are considered fatal threats to the social order. The novel is an indictment of consumer culture and the dangers it poses to personal integrity. It reveals the power of desire to transform and unhinge us, and the lengths to which we will go to get what we want. *Passing* is about hypocrisy and fear, secrecy and betrayal. It is a universal story of the messiness of being human as it is portrayed in the particularly explosive relationship between two black women, Clare Kendry and Irene Redfield.

Irene and Clare have not seen each other in twelve years

when they reunite by chance on the roof of the Drayton Hotel in Chicago, where both women are enjoying a respite from a blazing hot August day. The Drayton is an exclusive hotel, and not one in which African Americans, or Negroes, to use the parlance of the day, would be welcome. In fact, on the fateful day of their reunion, both women are passing for white.

In *Passing*, race is revealed to be, in part, a function of performance (the novel is structured in three sections—Encounter, Re-Encounter, Finale—much like acts in a theatrical piece), and blackness a matter of perception. Of the two women, it is Clare who appears to be so convincingly white that not only does Irene fail to identify Clare as a Negro, she doesn't recognize her childhood friend at all. Even after Clare introduces herself to Irene, Irene still doesn't recognize her or her blackness. When Clare uses her nickname, Irene searches her memory: "What white girls had she known well enough to have been familiarly addressed as 'Rene by them?" By contrast, Clare identifies Irene immediately. Irene squirms under Clare's unflinching stare, terrified of being seen for who she is, and also afraid of the embarrassment that would result from being ejected from the hotel. But even as she squirms, Irene cannot help but be aware of the exquisite beauty of the woman with the potent gaze.

It is only when Clare emits her distinctive laugh, which is "like the ringing of a delicate bell," that Irene finally recognizes her old friend. As the women talk, Clare appears more and more black to Irene. "Ah! Surely! They were Negro eyes! mysterious and concealing," she thinks as she feasts her own eyes upon Clare's stunning features. "There was about them something exotic," she thinks. As she is observing Clare, Irene is simultaneously making her up, inventing her—and inventing race, too. Clare isn't any more of a Negro after she reveals herself to Irene than she was before. As Irene confesses to another character later in the novel, no one can tell just by looking.

No one could tell by looking that Homer Plessy was black, either, when he stepped on a railroad car in New Orleans in 1892 in order to stage a legal challenge to the "separate but equal" doctrine. Not only did Plessy look white, he *was* white by any logical measure, claiming, as he did, only one-eighth black ancestry. He bought a first class ticket and boarded a "whites only" car unmolested; it was only because authorities had been alerted to his racial lineage that he was removed from the car. The argument made by Plessy's lawyers was that the overwhelming amount of white blood in his veins should make it possible for him to enjoy all the rights and entitlements of a white man. The overarching ambition of the argument, of course, was not to ensure the privileges of Homer Plessy as an individual, but to reveal the fallacious nature of racial categories in general. If he was seven-eighths white, what was it, exactly, that made him black?

The United States Supreme Court upheld the Louisiana Separate Car Act by an eight-to-one vote. Only one judge saw Plessy's point and was vocal about the absurdity of its implications. That dissenting voice belonged to Justice John Marshall Harlan, who wrote in his minority opinion of *Plessy v. Ferguson*:

> The destinies of the two races, in this country, are indissolubly linked together, and the interests of both require that the common government of all shall not permit the seeds of race hate to be planted under the sanction of law. What can more certainly arouse race hate, what more certainly create and perpetuate a feeling of distrust between these races than state enactments, which, in fact, proceed on the ground that colored citizens are so inferior and degraded that they cannot be allowed to sit in public coaches occupied by white citizens?

"Separate but equal" would be the principle that structured race relations in American society until *Brown v. Board of Education* in 1954.

Chicago, like New York in which the majority of the action in *Passing* is set, adopted laws prohibiting racial discrimination in public facilities in the late 1880s and early 1890s. But while African Americans may not have encountered de jure segregation in these cities, de facto segregation thrived, and the unwritten code of Jim Crow impacted the social fabric just as insidiously and profoundly as it did in the South, which explains Irene's anxiety about whether or not her blackness was showing as she sat on the roof of the Drayton.

According to the guidelines of genealogy, Clare's claims to blackness are nearly as tenuous as Homer Plessy's. Her grandfather was white. Her father was the product of her grandfather's dishonorable relationship with a black woman. Somewhere along the way, there had been money, but her grandfather squandered it. There is no mention in the novel of Clare's mother.

Once her father died, his pious aunts took Clare in, not as an expression of filial love but rather a sterile sense of Christian duty. They treated her like a servant, and forbade her from revealing the truth about her racial identity. Their bigotry was frank. "For all their Bibles and praying and ranting about honesty, they didn't want anyone to know that their darling brother had seduced—ruined, they called it—a Negro girl. They could excuse the ruin, but they couldn't forgive the tarbrush," Clare tells Irene. Clare was forbidden even to mention Negroes to the neighbors, much less discuss the South Side, where Irene and her friends lived in Chicago. It was easy for Clare to dispose of such an unhappy past, which was bankrupt of love as well as money.

As opposed to Homer Plessy, Clare Kendry has not used her fair skin to make a political statement; she has not been passing in order to undermine and subvert the system of white supremacy. There has been no greater good. Instead she has been passing purely for personal gain. Although she grew up in the same racial world as Irene, her social circumstances were radically different. Among their cohort of middle-class girls, "Clare had never been exactly one of the group." Her father had gone to college with some of the other girls' fathers, but he had somehow wound up a janitor, and "a very inefficient one at that." He was also a violent alcoholic who would ultimately die in a bar fight. Among Irene's earliest memories of Clare are images of "a pale small girl sitting on a ragged blue sofa, sewing pieces of bright red cloth together, while her drunken father, a tall, powerfully built man, raged threateningly up and down the shabby room, bellowing curses and making spasmodic lunges at her." The stubborn little girl boldly stitching together the bright cloth in defiance of her father's rage would grow into a young woman who defied fate, custom, and white supremacy by crossing the color line. But it wasn't racial self-hatred that catapulted Clare into whiteness; it was the shabby room. Clare passed for white because she hated being poor, not being black.

All passing narratives are about class as much as they are about race. One never passes down the social ladder; black characters become, or pose as, white in order to improve their material circumstances, or gain access in general to opportunities for personal, social, and professional advancement. The choice of individual comfort over the advancement of the race as a whole is always rendered as wrong; in most passing stories, material ambition and moral ruin are directly correlated. The anonymous narrator of *The Autobiography of an Ex-Colored Man* by James Weldon Johnson realizes that he has sold his birthright "for a mess of pottage" at the end of the novel in a moment of private revelation. By the time some passing subjects recognize the truly degraded implications of their decisions to engage in racial masquerade, it is too late. In the film *Imitation of Life*, the main character comes to her senses only after she finds out that her choice to pass has literally killed her mother. The denial of the black mother is often the surest sign of the low character of those who choose to pass. The narrator in the short story "Passing" by Langston Hughes gets a better job as a white man but his financial success requires him to ignore his own mother as they pass each other on the street. "That's the kind of thing that makes passing hard," the narrator sums up in a letter to his mother, "having to deny your own family when you see them."

If filial denial is required to secure the whiteness of the black character that would pass, often it is a longing for family that calls the passing subject home and back to blackness. In *Plum Bun* by Jessie Redmon Fauset, the main character Angela Murray, who passes for white, finally realizes that she can no longer tolerate the fact that passing for white has alienated her from her brown-skinned sister. When she comes out as black, the positive effect of her disclosure extends beyond her personal life. Unlike Angela, Clare has no family to miss, no black mother to deny, which makes it relatively easy for her, both practically and emotionally, to distance herself from her black past.

Clare Kendry is markedly different from other passing subjects in American literature. For one, she is not concerned with the moral implications of passing for white. Unlike other black characters whose passing enables them to marry white people, Clare does not pass for love. Even though she views passing through the lens of rank materialism, ultimately she sees passing as play. Clare Kendry is not an incarnation of the "tragic mulatto" figure, inherently alienated and adrift, whose mixed blood dooms her to racial purgatory. She is not wandering in the interstices of black and white. Instead, Clare is a hunter, stalking the margins of racial identity, hungry for forbidden experience, "stepping always on the edge of danger." She is a gambler, playing the high stakes game of racial roulette. For her, passing is a sport, and she is unrivaled in her technique.

Marrying a white person is an imperative in the literature of passing. If marrying white is not the endgame in and of itself, then the acquisition of white husbands and wives reveals the success of black characters in the general project of passing for white. There are white spouses who discover or are informed of the true racial identity of their passing romantic partners and love them anyway. The narrator of *The Autobiography of an Ex-Colored Man* confides his true racial heritage to the woman who will become his wife and waits anxiously for her verdict. She finally declares her love and then conveniently dies, taking his secret with her to the grave. Gertrude Martin in *Passing*, another childhood friend of Clare's, has a white husband who is apparently unbothered both by the fact that his wife is black and the possibility that their children may have brown skin. For a husband, however, Clare Kendry chooses not a sympathetic white man but an out-and-out racist.

"I don't dislike them, I hate them," says Clare's husband, Jack Bellew, in response to Irene's request that he clarify his true feelings about Negroes, or as Bellew refers to them, "black scrimy devils." He has no idea, while he delivers his racist diatribe, Irene reflects, that he is "sitting here surrounded by three black devils, drinking tea."

The devils in question are his wife Clare, Irene, and Gertrude Martin. Gertrude and Irene are understandably perturbed to find themselves in the precarious position of being in close proximity to such a man. Clare, however, enjoys the danger; Irene detects a "queer gleam" in her eye as she introduces her husband to her old friends. When she's had her fun, she calms his rage, wielding her irresistible charm like a tranquilizer gun, her smile softening and mellowing him "as the rays of the sun does a fruit."

Jack is wealthy and won Clare's hand with "untold gold" he acquired somehow in South America. Because her aunts demanded secrecy, he was not made aware of her racial background. He did, however, learn of the severity of her aunts and was presumably thrilled to make off with both the gold and the "blonde beauty out of the fairy-tale," as another white male character describes her. He was seduced by Clare's self-presentation as a damsel in distress, the same story that will similarly ensnare Irene, her husband Brian, and virtually everyone else with whom Clare comes in contact in *Passing*.

Clare is an artist—perhaps a con artist, but an artist all the same. We are introduced to her as a writer of passionate letters. ". . . For I am lonely, so lonely . . . cannot help longing to be with you again, as I have never longed for anything before." Her writing tools, purple ink and Italian paper, mark her as "mysterious" and "flaunting." She is obviously a consummate actor, having successfully passed for white for twelve years. Her most impressive instrument is her body, which she uses as a canvas. *Passing*, like Larsen's first novel *Quicksand*, is a sensual novel, and Clare is a sensory experience. In the opening scenes, she is a "sweetly scented woman in a fluttering dress of green chiffon whose mingled pattern of narcissuses, jonquils, and hyacinths was a reminder of pleasantly chill spring days." She is refreshment from the heat that Irene has just escaped. To see Clare is to experience her. Her gaze makes

Irene blush; her smile is like a caress. Being in Clare's presence makes Irene shiver. If Irene is initially unsettled by Clare's gaze, it is not long before it is Irene who can't keep her eyes off Clare.

Even when she begins to resent her presence, Irene is confounded and disarmed by the other woman's beauty, her "tempting mouth," "arresting eyes," and the luster of her skin. "Clare, exquisite, golden, fragrant, flaunting"—one nearly runs out of adjectives to describe her appeal. Viewed through Irene's eyes, Clare is the personification of desire itself. Even at the height of her annoyance with Clare, Irene finds herself seized by emotions she cannot control and grasps Clare's hands, blurting, "Dear God! But aren't you lovely, Clare!" All the scenes between the two women vibrate with a sexual tension so thick that Deborah McDowell and other critics have characterized *Passing* as a novel that is as much about the sexual longing between the two women as it is a story about race. Ann duCille suggests that readers imagine Clare as Irene's "alter libido, the buried, long-denied sexual self." Irene's need to repress her desire for Clare is so extreme that when she begins to entertain suspicions that Clare and her husband Brian are having an affair, it is possible to read her fears as a ruse she concocts in order to protect herself from her homosexual desires. Clare desires many things, among them to be among Negroes again. But ultimately, the true nature of her driving need is as opaque as the "ivory mask" she wears. What *is* transparent is Irene's fascination with Clare.

Clare is the most appealing character in the novel. There are other beautiful characters. Felise Freeland, a friend of Irene's and a woman with brown skin, is blessed with both "looks and brains," according to Irene. Certainly, Irene's appearance is pleasing to herself at least, if we are to judge by the amount of time she gazes at her reflection in the mirror. There are many cues in the novel to lead a reader to conclude that the entire social world that Brian and Irene inhabit is populated by pretty people. But Clare's beauty is of a different order. She is fundamentally dishonest, inarguably manipulative, yet she enchants every character, both minor and major, from the servants and children in the Redfield household to the glamorous Hugh Wentworth, who compares Clare to a "blonde beauty out of the fairy-tale." By association, Clare makes otherwise ignoble characteristics seem very attractive. She is not straightforward like Gertrude Martin, who claims she would have never married her husband without first revealing the truth about her racial identity. Gertrude may be honorable but she is not aspirational. Clare is rich; her husband is an international banking agent. Gertrude, whose husband is a butcher, looks "as if her husband might be a butcher," muses Irene. She is bland and broad; her hair has lost its curl. As opposed to Clare, who, when we first encounter her, is as vital as a garden, Gertrude stuffs her "stout legs" into "sleazy stockings of a vivid rose-beige shade." She has a bad manicure. "And she wasn't smoking."

Clare may not be aspirational as a woman who passes for white, but she represents the ambitions inherent in the ideal of the New Woman, a concept that emerged in the late nineteenth century and took hold of the American imagination in the wake of the industrial boom occasioned by World War I. The New Woman was the embodiment of first-wave feminist ideals. Also known as a flapper, she had a distinctive style that was a rejection of Victorian modes of dress and behavior. She bobbed her hair, drank cocktails, raised her hemlines, and danced in speakeasies. She thumbed her nose at gender conventions by questioning traditional marriage, sometimes wearing men's clothes, and smoking. She behaved as if she was the author of her own destiny. She spoke her mind, but she was largely composed by advertisers in the era of mass production.

"I've a good imagination," Clare says in response to Irene's curiosity about what she would have done if questioned about her ancestry during her life in the white world. She would have made something up, she insists, invented herself. But Clare is ultimately an invention of forces outside of her control. As a consummate New Woman, Clare Kendry is an emblem of the pleasures and dangers of material culture, in which even identities are disposable.

The New Woman had a sibling: the New Negro. They were

born at the same time and thrived as a result of the same historical shifts. Both are commonly considered under the cultural umbrella of the Jazz Age. The New Negro movement is often taken to be synonymous with the Harlem Renaissance, which would not have existed had it not been for the two million African Americans fleeing Southern poverty and racial violence between 1910–30. (Historian Daniel Sharfstein likens passing to racial migration.) But if the Harlem Renaissance is most often associated with art and performance, celebration and entertainment, the New Negro movement was a broader enterprise that encompassed these elements, but was even more importantly the name of the project of racial revision.

The New Negro movement was hardly new when it began. Since the inception of African presence in the United States, black people have been engaged in a drama of "re-presentation," an ongoing, endless struggle to redefine the image of the black in the white mind. During the Harlem Renaissance, the battle against stereotypes was most passionately fought on the landscape of New Negro literature. For African Americans, the written word has always provided both script and setting for racial redefinition and representation. In "The Dilemma of the Negro Author," James Weldon Johnson wrote: "The final measure of the greatness of all peoples is the amount and standard of the literature and art they have produced . . . And nothing will do more to change [the national mental attitude toward the Negro] and raise his status than a demonstration of intellectual parity by the Negro through the production of literature and art."

Within the ranks of New Negro writers, intellectuals, and artists, there was dissent. "We younger Negro artists who create now intend to express our individual dark-skinned selves without fear or shame. If white people are pleased we are glad. If they are not, it doesn't matter," wrote Langston Hughes in his 1926 essay "The Negro Artist and the Racial Mountain." "If colored people are pleased we are glad. If they are not, their displeasure doesn't matter either." Art required authenticity, and authenticity was incompatible with convention. "An artist must be free to choose what he does, certainly," Hughes wrote, "but he must also never be afraid to do what he must choose."

Like other younger Negro artists, Langston Hughes asserted his freedom through bold representations of sexuality, a sore spot for those bent on correcting stereotypes of black people as hypersexual. W. E. B. Du Bois, whom Hughes perhaps had in mind when he voiced disagreement with older Negro artists, summed up the root of the anxiety: "We are ashamed of sex and we lower our eyes when people talk of it. . . . Our worst side has been so shamelessly emphasized that we are denying we have or ever had a worst side. In all sorts of ways we are hemmed in and our new young artists have got to fight their way to freedom."

The value of freedom is something on which both generations of black artists could agree. Although he gave *Passing* a good review in *The Crisis*, Du Bois, who was editor of the magazine, did not note something obvious about the book, which is that Clare is, if nothing else, emblematic of the sex of which black people had been conditioned to feel ashamed. As a black woman who appears to be white, she is already sexualized; her body is evidence of sexual taboo. But Clare is also sexy. Her erotic arsenal includes a husky voice, a mouth like a "scarlet flower against the ivory of her skin," and a "trick of sliding down ivory lids over astonishing black eyes and then lifting them suddenly and turning on a caressing smile." Irene becomes flustered when the topic of sex comes up in her home (Junior has "picked up some queer ideas about things—some things—from the older boys," she tells her husband). Irene is a young woman in the novel, but she represents the older guard and its attitudes toward racial propriety, at least when it comes to Clare. Relative to her childhood friend, Irene is a conservative who is threatened by Clare because she represents a challenge to the sense of order and linear progress endemic to the "lifting as we climb" motto of the black bourgeoisie. "Her race! Race! The thing that bound and suffocated her." Irene wrings her hands as she contemplates betraying Clare by revealing her racial background to Jack in a desperate attempt to get rid of her.

The arguments espoused by race leaders Johnson and Du

Bois about the duties of black artists were reasonable and historically grounded. What Langston Hughes and Nella Larsen championed was emotion over reason, heart over head, pleasure instead of obligation. Irene is tied to race out of duty; Clare's relationship to blackness is affective. "You don't know, you can't realize how I want to see Negroes, to be with them again, to talk with them, to hear them laugh," Clare confesses to Irene. As a woman motivated by passion and excited to cross lines of propriety, Clare has a lot in common with the writer who dreamed her up: Nella Larsen.

Nella Larsen was born Nellie Walker in 1891 in Chicago. Her mother was a Danish immigrant and her father an immigrant from the Danish West Indies. Nella's father disappeared from her life when she was young. Her mother married a fellow Danish immigrant, Peter Larsen, with whom she had another child.

Like many fiction writers, Larsen incorporated elements of her own life into her writing. She shared with Clare the experience of being unwanted by white family members; neither Peter nor her half-sister acknowledged the ties that bound them. Like Clare, Nella was born poor and on the wrong side of town. Not only did Larsen spend her childhood in the vice district of Chicago, she was confronted by other dangers: a city in which the crossing of racial lines was unwelcome and cost those who disregarded them dearly. The rigid lines were officially underscored when, in 1920, the category "mulatto" was dropped from the census. There was no room for individuals whose bodies failed to conform to convention.

Nella was introduced to the world of the black bourgeoisie—the world in which Irene moved easily—when she was a student at Fisk University. There she bristled at the strict codes of dress and conduct. In her 1928 novel *Quicksand*, Larsen describes the disdain that the main character Helga Crane has toward the smug, insular world of the black elite at the fictional college of Naxos (an anagram for Saxon). "These people yapped loudly of race, of race consciousness, of race pride, and yet suppressed its most delightful manifestations, love of color, joy of rhythmic motion, naïve spontaneous laughter."

Ultimately Larsen was expelled from Fisk, most likely for violating dress code.

Larsen went from Fisk to Denmark, where she had spent time as a child. She returned to the United States and enrolled in nursing school, taking a position as head nurse at Tuskegee Institute in Alabama, the incarnation of the vision of Booker T. Washington, and along with Fisk, a model for Naxos. It was known as the "Tuskegee machine." In *Quicksand*, Helga reflects on her school: "This great community, she thought, was no longer a school. It had grown into a machine." Larsen found the working conditions at Tuskegee untenable. She resigned in 1916.

A few years later, she married Elmer Imes, who was at that point one of two African Americans to have ever held a PhD in physics. The couple moved to Harlem, where Larsen took a job at the 135th Street branch of the New York Public Library, now the Schomburg Center for Research in Black Culture. Soon her life as a writer would begin.

As Elmer's wife, Nella began to spend time with intellectual and cultural luminaries of the 1920s, black men like James Weldon Johnson, Walter White, and W. E. B. Du Bois. These men were architects of the Harlem Renaissance, authors of crucial philosophies that captured the concerns of black intellectuals of the moment. They were also central figures in the National Association for the Advancement of Colored People (NAACP), an organization for black progress that Du Bois helped to found in 1909. Irene Redfield, who prides herself on being a ticket taker for a ball for the Negro Welfare League, would have been impressed by the company Larsen kept.

The 135th Street library hosted events and speakers on a range of popular topics. Key Harlem Renaissance writers were part of these events as attendees or speakers, or were otherwise connected to the library. Larsen met Langston Hughes and Countee Cullen, whose 1925 poem "Heritage" she excerpted for the epitaph to *Passing*. She would share with the two men a close friend and ardent advocate, Carl Van Vechten.

A farsighted journalist, a best-selling novelist, an exquisite host, an exhaustive archivist, a prescient photographer, and one of the most controversial figures in the history of African American culture, Carl Van Vechten was one of Nella Larsen's best friends. She was acquainted with Van Vechten's reputation before she met him. He had been a celebrity in New York long before he began writing about black music and culture, but his recent publications in *Vanity Fair* had given him a particular status in black social circles. He and Larsen were drawn to each other immediately. Not only did their social worlds overlap, they shared the same taste for ribaldry and the same impatience with priggishness. Van Vechten would publish *Nigger Heaven* in 1926. The novel—and particularly its title— created a stir, drawing the ire of black and white readers for its sensational representations of black Harlem life. Mostly, however, the novel is a sober tale about the perils of artistic censorship for black writers.

Larsen admired Van Vechten's daring and also the excitement that attended the publication of *Nigger Heaven*. She wanted *Passing* to cause a sensation, too. "I have this day completed your novel 'Nig.' That is, it has only to be copied. Thank God, Glory Halleluja Amen!" Nella wrote to Carl in August 1928. Initially she was determined to use her title "Nig" to pay homage to Van Vechten's book. But the Knopfs, their mutual publishers, were bewildered by the outrage over the title of Van Vechten's novel and not interested in courting more controversy. Nella changed the title without a fuss, but she did dedicate the novel to Carl and his wife Fania, with whom she had also become close. She associated herself and her book with Van Vechten as much as possible. For an epigraph to the book, she used lines from Countee Cullen's poem "Heritage"; Van Vechten used a passage from the same poem as the epigraph for *Nigger Heaven*. She modeled a pivotal character in *Passing*, Hugh Wentworth, partly on Van Vechten. In a biographical statement she wrote for Knopf to use for publicity, she listed bridge and "collecting Van Vechteniana" as her hobbies.

Van Vechten adored *Passing*. He read it the same night that he received his copy and liked it so much he could barely sleep. The next morning, Carl brought the book with him to the

Knopf offices. "I stir Blanche & Alfred up about Nella Larsen's *Passing*, making quite a scene." He stopped at a florist to have flowers sent to Nella. Several days later, the marketing department at Knopf called him into a meeting with Larsen, and together they developed a strategy for selling the book that would showcase Van Vechten's enthusiasm. But neither the dedication nor the other forms of connection to Van Vechten set off an explosion for Larsen like the one Hughes had triggered by paying homage to Van Vechten in his 1927 poetry collection *Fine Clothes to the Jew*.

At least Floyd Calvin in the *Pittsburgh Courier* condemned *Passing* as a disgrace, which delighted Nella immensely. Both *Quicksand* and *Passing* received favorable reviews and garnered the respect of her New Negro peers.

Just as Larsen finished *Passing*, her marriage fell apart. She was a private person, and Van Vechten was one of very few people in whom she confided about her personal life. Her husband Elmer Imes did, too, and Van Vechten recorded visits from both distraught parties in his daybooks. The couple was in some financial trouble, and Elmer soon moved to Nashville to take a position at Fisk University, an institution to which Nella was not eager to return. Elmer would break his wife's heart by falling in love with another woman, the director of publicity and finance at Fisk, who was white, and a beloved member of the university community. Larsen still loved her husband and held on to the hope that they might reconcile, even as the strain of his affair affected her health. When the couple decided to separate, Elmer wrote to Van Vechten immediately, and asked that he counsel his soon to be ex-wife.

In the middle of her personal misfortune, and at the same time as she began to be recognized as a literary force among New Negro writers, Larsen was confronted with charges of plagiarism. A short story she had published in *The Forum*, "Sanctuary," bore unmistakable similarities to "Mrs. Adis," a story published eight years earlier by British writer Sheila Kaye-Smith. Larsen published a defense of her work as an original piece of fiction, but the shame of the accusations devastated her. Fortunately, Van Vechten took her side. He was, in fact, one of her only friends to defend her character while gossip about her spread throughout the black literary world.

About six years after the plagiarism scandal and three years after the salacious details of her divorce from Imes made the front page of the *Baltimore Afro-American* (including a rumor that she had jumped from a window in a suicide attempt), Larsen disappeared from the cultural world of black intellectuals and artists. No one was more devastated than Carl Van Vechten, who received the last piece of correspondence from Larsen in 1937, on his fifty-seventh birthday. For the rest of his life, Carl tried to reach Nella to discover some news about her through mutual friends (whom she had also cut off), but he never heard from her again. Larsen died in 1964 at the age of seventy-two, having spent her post–Harlem Renaissance years working as a nurse in a hospital on the Lower East Side of New York.

It is safe to say that both Nella Larsen and her character Clare Kendry would have had easier lives as mixed-race women in the twenty-first century. If the 1920 census, with its removal of "mulatto" as a viable racial category, officially erased the experience of being mixed-race in the United States, the inclusion on the 2000 census of categories that allow individuals to identify for the first time in history with more than one race has already generated new stories. According to the 2010 Census Brief, since 2000, the population reporting multiple races increased by 32 percent. Already, the structure of the new census has enabled people with complex racial backgrounds to more aptly define themselves.

Unfortunately, the script had already been written for Clare. She was a woman who insisted on being free, and she paid for the crime of her hunger not only to defy racial convention but also the customs of gender, as well. The men in the novel are world explorers, or yearn to be: Jack Bellew is an international banker; Hugh Wentworth has "lived on edges of nowhere in at least three continents"; Brian Redfield longs to abandon American racism and move to Brazil. Clare is the true adventurer, however. Her wanderlust is domestic but perhaps more dangerous in that it is not structured by travel or outlined in a map but rather a function of her everyday life. Her literary descendants, such as Janie Crawford in *Their Eyes Were Watching God* by Zora Neale Hurston; Sula in the eponymous novel by Toni Morrison; Birdie in *Caucasia* by Danzy Senna; and the protagonists in *Interesting Women* by Andrea Lee, also live dangerously by pushing the boundaries of social convention. But in the high stakes games that Clare plays in 1929, the house always wins.

"What is Africa to me?" muses the speaker in "Heritage." Where does race reside? In blood, ancestry, or emotion? How can it be identified, much less quantified? Is it absurdity or a mystery? Race is a function of law, history, and politics, not science. Yet there is an ineffable quality to blackness, a mysterious factor that drives Clare to risk everything in order to "see Negroes, to be with them again, to talk with them, to hear them laugh."

It is this ineffability, the mystery that Clare embodies, that Irene cannot bear. She curses race as a yoke, but what she ultimately rejects is not a racial bond with Clare, but the awareness that identity itself is transitional, as mobile as the trains that made it possible for millions of African Americans to leave the South during the Great Migration, and the railroad car that provided the platform for Homer Plessy's historic confrontation. The self itself is unstable, just like the concept of race.

At the end of the novel, Irene finishes her final cigarette and throws it out of a window, "watching the tiny spark drop slowly down to the white ground below." It is impossible not to associate the cigarette sparks with the vitality and danger that Clare brought into her life. But Clare Kendry is unforgettable. After all, when a fire goes out, one does not necessarily remember the ashes. But one certainly remembers the brilliance of the flame.

EMILY BERNARD

SUGGESTIONS FOR FURTHER READING

Bernard, Emily. *Carl Van Vechten and the Harlem Renaissance: A Portrait in Black and White.* New Haven: Yale University Press, 2012.

Bennett, Juda. *The Passing Figure: Racial Confusion in Modern American Literature.* New York: Peter Lang, 1996.

Berzon, Judith R. *Neither White Nor Black: The Mulatto Character in American Fiction.* New York: New York University Press, 1978.

Carby, Hazel V. *Reconstructing Womanhood: The Emergence of the Afro-American Woman Novelist.* New York: Oxford University Press, 1987.

Caughie, Pamela L. *Passing and Pedagogy: The Dynamics of Responsibility.* Urbana-Champaign: University of Illinois Press, 1999.

Davis, Thadious M. *Nella Larsen, Novelist of the Harlem Renaissance: A Woman's Life Unveiled.* Baton Rouge: Louisiana State University Press, 1994.

duCille, Ann. *The Coupling Convention: Sex, Text, and Tradition in Black Women's Fiction.* New York: Oxford University Press, 1993.

Hobbs, Allyson. *A Chosen Exile: A History of Racial Passing in American Life.* Cambridge: Harvard University Press, 2016.

Huggins, Nathan Irvin. *Harlem Renaissance.* New York: Oxford University Press, 1971.

Hutchinson, George. *In Search of Nella Larsen: A Biography of the Color Line.* Cambridge: Harvard University Press, 2006.

Kaplan, Carla. *Passing: Nella Larsen.* Norton Critical Editions: Authoritative Text Backgrounds and Contexts Criticism. New York: W. W. Norton & Company, 2007.

Larson, Charles R. *Invisible Darkness: Jean Toomer & Nella Larsen.* Iowa City: University of Iowa Press, 1993.

Lewis, David Levering. *When Harlem Was In Vogue.* New York: Vintage Books, 1982.

McClendon, Jacquelyn Y. *The Politics of Color in the Fiction of Jessie Fauset and Nella Larsen.* Charlottesville: University of Virginia Press, 1995.

Pfeiffer, Kathleen. *Race Passing and American Individualism.* Amherst: University of Massachusetts Press, 2003.

Sharfstein, Daniel J. *The Invisible Line: A Secret History of Race in America.* New York: Penguin, 2011.

Smith-Pryor, Elizabeth M. *Property Rites: The Rhinelander Trial, Passing, and the Protection of Whiteness.* Chapel Hill: University of North Carolina Press, 2009.

Sollors, Werner. *Neither Black nor White yet Both: Thematic Explorations of Interracial Literature.* Cambridge: Harvard University Press, 1999.

Wilkerson, Isabel. *The Warmth of Other Suns: The Epic Story of America's Great Migration.* New York: Vintage, 2011.

Zeitz, Joshua. *Flapper: A Madcap Story of Sex, Style, Celebrity, and the Women Who Made America Modern.* New York: Broadway Books, 2007.

A NOTE ON THE TEXT

The text of this edition is based on the first edition, first printing of *Passing*, which was published by Alfred A. Knopf in 1929. The first printing of the first edition included a brief final paragraph that was dropped in the third printing of the novel: "Centuries after, she heard the strange man saying: 'Death by misadventure, I'm inclined to believe. Let's go up and have another look at that window.'" Although it is possible that the revised ending conformed to the author's sense of her novel, there is no indication that Nella Larsen herself recommended, sought, or approved the excision of the final paragraph. The text of this edition, therefore, follows the original Knopf first printing.

With the exception of a few minor typographical errors, which have been silently corrected, the original punctuation, spelling, and division of words, such as "kerb," "favourite," "for ever," and "week end," have been retained throughout this text.

PASSING

FOR
Carl Van Vechten[1]
AND
Fania Marinoff[2]

One three centuries removed
From the scenes his fathers loved,
Spicy grove, cinnamon tree,
What is Africa to me?[1]

—COUNTÉE CULLEN[2]

PART ONE

ENCOUNTER

ONE

It was the last letter in Irene Redfield's little pile of morning mail. After her other ordinary and clearly directed letters the long envelope of thin Italian paper with its almost illegible scrawl seemed out of place and alien. And there was, too, something mysterious and slightly furtive about it. A thin sly thing which bore no return address to betray the sender. Not that she hadn't immediately known who its sender was. Some two years ago she had one very like it in outward appearance. Furtive, but yet in some peculiar, determined way a little flaunting. Purple ink. Foreign paper of extraordinary size.

It had been, Irene noted, postmarked in New York the day before. Her brows came together in a tiny frown. The frown, however, was more from perplexity than from annoyance; though there was in her thoughts an element of both. She was wholly unable to comprehend such an attitude towards danger as she was sure the letter's contents would reveal; and she disliked the idea of opening and reading it.

This, she reflected, was of a piece with all that she knew of Clare Kendry. Stepping always on the edge of danger. Always aware, but not drawing back or turning aside. Certainly not because of any alarms or feeling of outrage on the part of others.

And for a swift moment Irene Redfield seemed to see a pale small girl sitting on a ragged blue sofa, sewing pieces of bright red cloth together, while her drunken father, a tall, powerfully built man, raged threateningly up and down the shabby room, bellowing curses and making spasmodic lunges at her which were not the less frightening because they were, for the most part, ineffectual. Sometimes he did manage to reach her. But only the fact that the child had edged herself and her poor sewing over to the farthermost corner of the sofa suggested that she was in any way perturbed by this menace to herself and her work.

Clare had known well enough that it was unsafe to take a portion of the dollar that was her weekly wage for the doing of many errands for the dressmaker who lived on the top floor of the building of which Bob Kendry was janitor. But that knowledge had not deterred her. She wanted to go to her Sunday school's picnic, and she had made up her mind to wear a new dress. So, in spite of certain unpleasantness and possible danger, she had taken the money to buy the material for that pathetic little red frock.

There had been, even in those days, nothing sacrificial in Clare Kendry's idea of life, no allegiance beyond her own immediate desire. She was selfish, and cold, and hard. And yet she had, too, a strange capacity of transforming warmth and passion, verging sometimes almost on theatrical heroics.

Irene, who was a year or more older than Clare, remembered the day that Bob Kendry had been brought home dead, killed in a silly saloon-fight. Clare, who was at that time a scant fifteen years old, had just stood there with her lips pressed together, her thin arms folded across her narrow chest, staring down at the familiar pasty-white face of her parent with a sort of disdain in her slanting black eyes. For a very long time she had stood like that, silent and staring. Then, quite suddenly, she had given way to a torrent of weeping, swaying her thin body, tearing at her bright hair, and stamping her small feet. The outburst had ceased as suddenly as it had begun. She glanced quickly about the bare room, taking everyone in, even the two policemen, in a sharp look of flashing scorn. And, in the next instant, she had turned and vanished through the door.

Seen across the long stretch of years, the thing had more the appearance of an outpouring of pent-up fury than of an overflow of grief for her dead father; though she had been, Irene admitted, fond enough of him in her own rather catlike way.

Catlike. Certainly that was the word which best described Clare Kendry, if any single word could describe her. Sometimes she was hard and apparently without feeling at all; sometimes she was affectionate and rashly impulsive. And there was about her an amazing soft malice, hidden well away until provoked. Then she was capable of scratching, and very effectively too. Or, driven to anger, she would fight with a ferocity and impetuousness that disregarded or forgot any danger; superior strength, numbers, or other unfavourable circumstances. How savagely she had clawed those boys the day they had hooted her parent and sung a derisive rhyme, of their own composing, which pointed out certain eccentricities in his careening gait! And how deliberately she had—

Irene brought her thoughts back to the present, to the letter from Clare Kendry that she still held unopened in her hand. With a little feeling of apprehension, she very slowly cut the envelope, drew out the folded sheets, spread them, and began to read.

It was, she saw at once, what she had expected since learning from the postmark that Clare was in the city. An extravagantly phrased wish to see her again. Well, she needn't and wouldn't, Irene told herself, accede to that. Nor would she assist Clare to realize her foolish desire to return for a moment to that life which long ago, and of her own choice, she had left behind her.

She ran through the letter, puzzling out, as best she could, the carelessly formed words or making instinctive guesses at them.

". . . For I am lonely, so lonely . . . cannot help longing to be with you again, as I have never longed for anything before; and I have wanted many things in my life. . . . You can't know how in this pale life of mine I am all the time seeing the bright pictures of that other that I once thought I was glad to be free of. . . . It's like an ache, a pain that never ceases. . . ." Sheets upon thin sheets of it. And ending finally with, "and it's your fault, 'Rene dear. At least partly. For I wouldn't now, perhaps, have this terrible, this wild desire if I hadn't seen you that time in Chicago. . . ."

Brilliant red patches flamed in Irene Redfield's warm olive cheeks.

"That time in Chicago." The words stood out from among the many paragraphs of other words, bringing with them a clear, sharp remembrance, in which even now, after two years, humiliation, resentment, and rage were mingled.

TWO

This is what Irene Redfield remembered.

Chicago. August. A brilliant day, hot, with a brutal staring sun pouring down rays that were like molten rain. A day on which the very outlines of the buildings shuddered as if in protest at the heat. Quivering lines sprang up from baked pavements and wriggled along the shining car-tracks.[1] The automobiles parked at the kerbs were a dancing blaze, and the glass of the shop-windows threw out a blinding radiance. Sharp particles of dust rose from the burning sidewalks, stinging the seared or dripping skins of wilting pedestrians. What small breeze there was seemed like the breath of a flame fanned by slow bellows.

It was on that day of all others that Irene set out to shop for the things which she had promised to take home from Chicago to her two small sons, Brian junior and Theodore. Characteristically, she had put it off until only a few crowded days remained of her long visit. And only this sweltering one was free of engagements till the evening.

Without too much trouble she had got the mechanical aeroplane for Junior. But the drawing-book, for which Ted had so gravely and insistently given her precise directions, had sent her in and out of five shops without success.

It was while she was on her way to a sixth place that right before her smarting eyes a man toppled over and became an inert crumpled heap on the scorching cement. About the lifeless figure a little crowd gathered. Was the man dead, or only faint? someone asked her. But Irene didn't know and didn't try to discover. She edged her way out of the increasing crowd, feeling disagreeably damp and sticky and soiled from contact with so many sweating bodies.

For a moment she stood fanning herself and dabbing at her moist face with an inadequate scrap of handkerchief. Suddenly she was aware that the whole street had a wobbly look, and realized that she was about to faint. With a quick perception of the need for immediate safety, she lifted a wavering hand in the direction of a cab parked directly in front of her. The perspiring driver jumped out and guided her to his car. He helped, almost lifted her in. She sank down on the hot leather seat.

For a minute her thoughts were nebulous. They cleared.

"I guess," she told her Samaritan, "it's tea I need. On a roof somewhere."

"The Drayton,[2] ma'am?" he suggested. "They do say as how it's always a breeze up there."

"Thank you. I think the Drayton'll do nicely," she told him.

There was that little grating sound of the clutch being slipped in as the man put the car in gear and slid deftly out into the boiling traffic. Reviving under the warm breeze stirred up by the moving cab, Irene made some small attempts to repair the damage that the heat and crowds had done to her appearance.

All too soon the rattling vehicle shot towards the sidewalk and stood still. The driver sprang out and opened the door before the hotel's decorated attendant could reach it. She got out, and thanking him smilingly as well as in a more substantial manner for his kind helpfulness and understanding, went in through the Drayton's wide doors.

Stepping out of the elevator that had brought her to the roof, she was led to a table just in front of a long window whose gently moving curtains suggested a cool breeze. It was, she thought, like being wafted upward on a magic carpet to another world, pleasant, quiet, and strangely remote from the sizzling one that she had left below.

The tea, when it came, was all that she had desired and expected. In fact, so much was it what she had desired and expected that after the first deep cooling drink she was able to forget it, only now and then sipping, a little absently, from the tall green glass, while she surveyed the room about her or looked out over some lower buildings at the bright unstirred blue of the lake reaching away to an undetected horizon.

She had been gazing down for some time at the specks of cars and people creeping about in streets, and thinking how silly they looked, when on taking up her glass she was surprised to find it empty at last. She asked for more tea and while she waited, began to recall the happenings of the day and to wonder what she was to do about Ted and his book. Why was it that almost invariably he wanted something that was difficult or impossible to get? Like his father. For ever wanting something that he couldn't have.

Presently there were voices, a man's booming one and a woman's slightly husky. A waiter passed her, followed by a sweetly scented woman in a fluttering dress of green chiffon whose mingled pattern of narcissuses, jonquils, and hyacinths was a reminder of pleasantly chill spring days. Behind her there was a man, very red in the face, who was mopping his neck and forehead with a big crumpled handkerchief.

"Oh dear!" Irene groaned, rasped by annoyance, for after a little discussion and commotion they had stopped at the very next table. She had been alone there at the window and it had been so satisfyingly quiet. Now, of course, they would chatter.

But no. Only the woman sat down. The man remained standing, abstractedly pinching the knot of his bright blue tie. Across the small space that separated the two tables his voice carried clearly.

"See you later, then," he declared, looking down at the woman. There was pleasure in his tones and a smile on his face.

His companion's lips parted in some answer, but her words were blurred by the little intervening distance and the medley of noises floating up from the streets below. They didn't reach Irene. But she noted the peculiar caressing smile that accompanied them.

The man said: "Well, I suppose I'd better," and smiled again, and said good-bye, and left.

An attractive-looking woman, was Irene's opinion, with

those dark, almost black, eyes and that wide mouth like a
scarlet flower against the ivory of her skin. Nice clothes too,
just right for the weather, thin and cool without being mussy,
as summer things were so apt to be.

A waiter was taking her order. Irene saw her smile up at him
as she murmured something—thanks, maybe. It was an odd
sort of smile. Irene couldn't quite define it, but she was sure
that she would have classed it, coming from another woman,
as being just a shade too provocative for a waiter. About this
one, however, there was something that made her hesitate to
name it that. A certain impression of assurance, perhaps.

The waiter came back with the order. Irene watched her
spread out her napkin, saw the silver spoon in the white hand
slit the dull gold of the melon. Then, conscious that she had
been staring, she looked quickly away.

Her mind returned to her own affairs. She had settled, definitely, the problem of the proper one of two frocks for the
bridge party that night, in rooms whose atmosphere would be
so thick and hot that every breath would be like breathing
soup. The dress decided, her thoughts had gone back to the
snag of Ted's book, her unseeing eyes far away on the lake,
when by some sixth sense she was acutely aware that someone
was watching her.

Very slowly she looked around, and into the dark eyes of
the woman in the green frock at the next table. But she evidently failed to realize that such intense interest as she was
showing might be embarrassing, and continued to stare. Her
demeanour was that of one who with utmost singleness of
mind and purpose was determined to impress firmly and accurately each detail of Irene's features upon her memory for
all time, nor showed the slightest trace of disconcertment at
having been detected in her steady scrutiny.

Instead, it was Irene who was put out. Feeling her colour
heighten under the continued inspection, she slid her eyes
down. What, she wondered, could be the reason for such persistent attention? Had she, in her haste in the taxi, put her hat
on backwards? Guardedly she felt at it. No. Perhaps there was
a streak of powder somewhere on her face. She made a quick

pass over it with her handkerchief. Something wrong with her dress? She shot a glance over it. Perfectly all right. *What* was it?

Again she looked up, and for a moment her brown eyes politely returned the stare of the other's black ones, which never for an instant fell or wavered. Irene made a little mental shrug. Oh well, let her look! She tried to treat the woman and her watching with indifference, but she couldn't. All her efforts to ignore her, it, were futile. She stole another glance. Still looking. What strange languorous eyes she had!

And gradually there rose in Irene a small inner disturbance, odious and hatefully familiar. She laughed softly, but her eyes flashed.

Did that woman, could that woman, somehow know that here before her very eyes on the roof of the Drayton sat a Negro?

Absurd! Impossible! White people were so stupid about such things for all that they usually asserted that they were able to tell; and by the most ridiculous means, finger-nails, palms of hands, shapes of ears, teeth, and other equally silly rot. They always took her for an Italian, a Spaniard, a Mexican, or a gipsy. Never, when she was alone, had they even remotely seemed to suspect that she was a Negro. No, the woman sitting there staring at her couldn't possibly know.

Nevertheless, Irene felt, in turn, anger, scorn, and fear slide over her. It wasn't that she was ashamed of being a Negro, or even of having it declared. It was the idea of being ejected from any place, even in the polite and tactful way in which the Drayton would probably do it, that disturbed her.

But she looked, boldly this time, back into the eyes still frankly intent upon her. They did not seem to her hostile or resentful. Rather, Irene had the feeling that they were ready to smile if she would. Nonsense, of course. The feeling passed, and she turned away with the firm intention of keeping her gaze on the lake, the roofs of the buildings across the way, the sky, anywhere but on that annoying woman. Almost immediately, however, her eyes were back again. In the midst of her fog of uneasiness she had been seized by a desire to outstare the rude observer. Suppose the woman did know or suspect her race. She couldn't prove it.

Suddenly her small fright increased. Her neighbour had risen and was coming towards her. What was going to happen now?

"Pardon me," the woman said pleasantly, "but I think I know you." Her slightly husky voice held a dubious note.

Looking up at her, Irene's suspicions and fears vanished. There was no mistaking the friendliness of that smile or resisting its charm. Instantly she surrendered to it and smiled too, as she said: "I'm afraid you're mistaken."

"Why, of course, I know you!" the other exclaimed. "Don't tell me you're not Irene Westover. Or do they still call you 'Rene?"

In the brief second before her answer, Irene tried vainly to recall where and when this woman could have known her. There, in Chicago. And before her marriage. That much was plain. High school? College? Y. W. C. A. committees? High school, most likely. What white girls had she known well enough to have been familiarly addressed as 'Rene by them? The woman before her didn't fit her memory of any of them. Who was she?

"Yes, I'm Irene Westover. And though nobody calls me 'Rene any more, it's good to hear the name again. And you—" She hesitated, ashamed that she could not remember, and hoping that the sentence would be finished for her.

"Don't you know me? Not really, 'Rene?"

"I'm sorry, but just at the minute I can't seem to place you."

Irene studied the lovely creature standing beside her for some clue to her identity. Who could she be? Where and when had they met? And through her perplexity there came the thought that the trick which her memory had played her was for some reason more gratifying than disappointing to her old acquaintance, that she didn't mind not being recognized.

And, too, Irene felt that she was just about to remember her. For about the woman was some quality, an intangible something, too vague to define, too remote to seize, but which was, to Irene Redfield, very familiar. And that voice. Surely she'd heard those husky tones somewhere before. Perhaps before time, contact, or something had been at them, making them into a voice remotely suggesting England. Ah! Could it have been in Europe that they had met? 'Rene. No.

"Perhaps," Irene began, "you—"

The woman laughed, a lovely laugh, a small sequence of notes that was like a trill and also like the ringing of a delicate bell fashioned of a precious metal, a tinkling.

Irene drew a quick sharp breath. "Clare!" she exclaimed, "not really Clare Kendry?"

So great was her astonishment that she had started to rise.

"No, no, don't get up," Clare Kendry commanded, and sat down herself. "You've simply got to stay and talk. We'll have something more. Tea? Fancy meeting you here! It's simply too, too lucky!"

"It's awfully surprising," Irene told her, and, seeing the change in Clare's smile, knew that she had revealed a corner of her own thoughts. But she only said: "I'd never in this world have known you if you hadn't laughed. You are changed, you know. And yet, in a way, you're just the same."

"Perhaps," Clare replied. "Oh, just a second."

She gave her attention to the waiter at her side. "M-mm, let's see. Two teas. And bring some cigarettes. Y-es, they'll be all right. Thanks." Again that odd upward smile. Now, Irene was sure that it was too provocative for a waiter.

While Clare had been giving the order, Irene made a rapid mental calculation. It must be, she figured, all of twelve years since she, or anybody that she knew, had laid eyes on Clare Kendry.

After her father's death she'd gone to live with some relatives, aunts or cousins two or three times removed, over on the west side: relatives that nobody had known the Kendrys' possessed until they had turned up at the funeral and taken Clare away with them.

For about a year or more afterwards she would appear occasionally among her old friends and acquaintances on the south side for short little visits that were, they understood, always stolen from the endless domestic tasks in her new home. With each succeeding one she was taller, shabbier, and more belligerently sensitive. And each time the look on her face was more resentful and brooding. "I'm worried about Clare, she seems so unhappy," Irene remembered her mother saying. The visits dwindled, becoming shorter, fewer, and further apart until at last they ceased.

Irene's father, who had been fond of Bob Kendry, made a special trip over to the west side about two months after the last time Clare had been to see them and returned with the bare information that he had seen the relatives and that Clare had disappeared. What else he had confided to her mother, in the privacy of their own room, Irene didn't know.

But she had had something more than a vague suspicion of its nature. For there had been rumours. Rumours that were, to girls of eighteen and nineteen years, interesting and exciting.

There was the one about Clare Kendry's having been seen at the dinner hour in a fashionable hotel in company with another woman and two men, all of them white. And *dressed!* And there was another which told of her driving in Lincoln Park[3] with a man, unmistakably white, and evidently rich. Packard limousine,[4] chauffeur in livery, and all that. There had been others whose context Irene could no longer recollect, but all pointing in the same glamorous direction.

And she could remember quite vividly how, when they used to repeat and discuss these tantalizing stories about Clare, the girls would always look knowingly at one another and then, with little excited giggles, drag away their eager shining eyes and say with lurking undertones of regret or disbelief some such thing as: "Oh, well, maybe she's got a job or something," or "After all, it mayn't have been Clare," or "You can't believe all you hear."

And always some girl, more matter-of-fact or more frankly malicious than the rest, would declare: "Of course it was Clare! Ruth said it was and so did Frank, and they certainly know her when they see her as well as we do." And someone else would say: "Yes, you can bet it was Clare all right." And then they would all join in asserting that there could be no mistake about it's having been Clare, and that such circumstances could mean only one thing. Working indeed! People didn't take their servants to the Shelby[5] for dinner. Certainly not all dressed up like that. There would follow insincere regrets, and somebody would say: "Poor girl, I suppose it's true enough, but what can you expect. Look at her father. And her mother, they say, would have run away if she hadn't died. Besides, Clare always had a—a—having way with her."

Precisely that! The words came to Irene as she sat there on the Drayton roof, facing Clare Kendry. "A having way." Well, Irene acknowledged, judging from her appearance and manner, Clare seemed certainly to have succeeded in having a few of the things that she wanted.

It was, Irene repeated, after the interval of the waiter, a great surprise and a very pleasant one to see Clare again after all those years, twelve at least.

"Why, Clare, you're the last person in the world I'd have expected to run into. I guess that's why I didn't know you."

Clare answered gravely: "Yes. It is twelve years. But I'm not surprised to see you, 'Rene. That is, not so very. In fact, ever since I've been here, I've more or less hoped that I should, or someone. Preferably you, though. Still, I imagine that's because I've thought of you often and often, while you—I'll wager you've never given me a thought."

It was true, of course. After the first speculations and indictments, Clare had gone completely from Irene's thoughts. And from the thoughts of others too—if their conversation was any indication of their thoughts.

Besides, Clare had never been exactly one of the group, just as she'd never been merely the janitor's daughter, but the daughter of Mr. Bob Kendry, who, it was true, was a janitor, but who also, it seemed, had been in college with some of their fathers. Just how or why he happened to be a janitor, and a very inefficient one at that, they none of them quite knew. One of Irene's brothers, who had put the question to their father, had been told: "That's something that doesn't concern you," and given him the advice to be careful not to end in the same manner as "poor Bob."

No, Irene hadn't thought of Clare Kendry. Her own life had been too crowded. So, she supposed, had the lives of other people. She defended her—their—forgetfulness. "You know how it is. Everybody's so busy. People leave, drop out, maybe for a little while there's talk about them, or questions; then, gradually they're forgotten."

"Yes, that's natural," Clare agreed. And what, she inquired, had they said of her for that little while at the beginning before they'd forgotten her altogether?

Irene looked away. She felt the telltale colour rising in her cheeks. "You can't," she evaded, "expect me to remember trifles like that over twelve years of marriages, births, deaths, and the war."

There followed that trill of notes that was Clare Kendry's laugh, small and clear and the very essence of mockery.

"Oh, 'Rene!" she cried, "of course you remember! But I won't make you tell me, because I know just as well as if I'd been there and heard every unkind word. Oh, I know, I know. Frank Danton saw me in the Shelby one night. Don't tell me he didn't broadcast that, and with embroidery. Others may have seen me at other times. I don't know. But once I met Margaret Hammer in Marshall Field's.[6] I'd have spoken, was on the very point of doing it, but she cut me dead. My dear 'Rene, I assure you that from the way she looked through me, even I was uncertain whether I was actually there in the flesh or not. I remember it clearly, too clearly. It was that very thing which, in a way, finally decided me not to go out and see you one last time before I went away to stay. Somehow, good as all of you, the whole family, had always been to the poor forlorn child that was me, I felt I shouldn't be able to bear that. I mean if any of you, your mother or the boys or— Oh, well, I just felt I'd rather not know it if you did. And so I stayed away. Silly, I suppose. Sometimes I've been sorry I didn't go."

Irene wondered if it was tears that made Clare's eyes so luminous.

"And now 'Rene, I want to hear all about you and everybody and everything. You're married, I s'pose?"

Irene nodded.

"Yes," Clare said knowingly, "you would be. Tell me about it."

And so for an hour or more they had sat there smoking and drinking tea and filling in the gap of twelve years with talk. That is, Irene did. She told Clare about her marriage and removal to New York, about her husband, and about her two sons, who were having their first experience of being separated from their parents at a summer camp, about her mother's death, about the marriages of her two brothers. She told of the marriages, births and deaths in other families that Clare had known, opening up, for her, new vistas on the lives of old friends and acquaintances.

Clare drank it all in, these things which for so long she had wanted to know and hadn't been able to learn. She sat motionless, her bright lips slightly parted, her whole face lit by the radiance of her happy eyes. Now and then she put a question, but for the most part she was silent.

Somewhere outside, a clock struck. Brought back to the present, Irene looked down at her watch and exclaimed: "Oh, I must go, Clare!"

A moment passed during which she was the prey of uneasiness. It had suddenly occurred to her that she hadn't asked Clare anything about her own life and that she had a very definite unwillingness to do so. And she was quite well aware of the reason for that reluctance. But, she asked herself, wouldn't it, all things considered, be the kindest thing not to ask? If things with Clare were as she—as they all—had suspected, wouldn't it be more tactful to seem to forget to inquire how she had spent those twelve years?

If? It was that "if" which bothered her. It might be, it might just be, in spite of all gossip and even appearances to the contrary, that there was nothing, had been nothing, that couldn't be simply and innocently explained. Appearances, she knew now, had a way sometimes of not fitting facts, and if Clare hadn't—Well, if they had all been wrong, then certainly she ought to express some interest in what had happened to her.

It would seem queer and rude if she didn't. But how was she to know? There was, she at last decided, no way; so she merely said again: "I must go, Clare."

"Please, not so soon, 'Rene," Clare begged, not moving.

Irene thought: "She's really almost too good-looking. It's hardly any wonder that she—"

"And now, 'Rene dear, that I've found you, I mean to see lots and lots of you. We're here for a month at least. Jack, that's my husband, is here on business. Poor dear! in this heat. Isn't it beastly? Come to dinner with us tonight, won't you?" And she gave Irene a curious little sidelong glance and a sly, ironical smile peeped out on her full red lips, as if she had been in the secret of the other's thoughts and was mocking her.

Irene was conscious of a sharp intake of breath, but whether it was relief or chagrin that she felt, she herself could not have told. She said hastily: "I'm afraid I can't, Clare. I'm filled up. Dinner and bridge. I'm so sorry."

"Come tomorrow instead, to tea," Clare insisted. "Then you'll see Margery—she's just ten—and Jack too, maybe, if he hasn't got an appointment or something."

From Irene came an uneasy little laugh. She had an engagement for tomorrow also and she was afraid that Clare would not believe it. Suddenly, now, that possibility disturbed her. Therefore it was with a half-vexed feeling at the sense of undeserved guilt that had come upon her that she explained that it wouldn't be possible because she wouldn't be free for tea, or for luncheon or dinner either. "And the next day's Friday when I'll be going away for the week-end, Idlewild,[7] you know. It's quite the thing now." And then she had an inspiration.

"Clare!" she exclaimed, "why don't you come up with me? Our place is probably full up—Jim's wife has a way of collecting mobs of the most impossible people—but we can always manage to find room for one more. And you'll see absolutely everybody."

In the very moment of giving the invitation she regretted it. What a foolish, what an idiotic impulse to have given way to! She groaned inwardly as she thought of the endless explanations in which it would involve her, of the curiosity, and the

talk, and the lifted eyebrows. It wasn't she assured herself, that
she was a snob, that she cared greatly for the petty restrictions
and distinctions with which what called itself Negro society
chose to hedge itself about; but that she had a natural and
deeply rooted aversion to the kind of front-page notoriety that
Clare Kendry's presence in Idlewild, as her guest, would expose her to. And here she was, perversely and against all reason, inviting her.

But Clare shook her head. "Really, I'd love to, 'Rene," she
said, a little mournfully. "There's nothing I'd like better. But
I couldn't. I mustn't, you see. It wouldn't do at all. I'm sure
you understand. I'm simply crazy to go, but I can't." The dark
eyes glistened and there was a suspicion of a quaver in the
husky voice. "And believe me, 'Rene, I do thank you for asking me. Don't think I've entirely forgotten just what it would
mean for you if I went. That is, if you still care about such
things."

All indication of tears had gone from her eyes and voice,
and Irene Redfield, searching her face, had an offended feeling
that behind what was now only an ivory mask lurked a scornful amusement. She looked away, at the wall far beyond Clare.
Well, she deserved it, for, as she acknowledged to herself, she
was relieved. And for the very reason at which Clare had
hinted. The fact that Clare had guessed her perturbation did
not, however, in any degree lessen that relief. She was annoyed
at having been detected in what might seem to be an insincer-
ity; but that was all.

The waiter came with Clare's change. Irene reminded herself
that she ought immediately to go. But she didn't move.

The truth was, she was curious. There were things that she
wanted to ask Clare Kendry. She wished to find out about this
hazardous business of "passing," this breaking away from all
that was familiar and friendly to take one's chance in another
environment, not entirely strange, perhaps, but certainly not
entirely friendly. What, for example, one did about background, how one accounted for oneself. And how one felt when
one came into contact with other Negroes. But she couldn't.
She was unable to think of a single question that in its context

or its phrasing was not too frankly curious, if not actually impertinent.

As if aware of her desire and her hesitation, Clare remarked, thoughtfully: "You know, 'Rene, I've often wondered why more coloured girls, girls like you and Margaret Hammer and Esther Dawson and—oh, lots of others—never 'passed' over. It's such a frightfully easy thing to do. If one's the type, all that's needed is a little nerve."

"What about background? Family, I mean. Surely you can't just drop down on people from nowhere and expect them to receive you with open arms, can you?"

"Almost," Clare asserted. "You'd be surprised, 'Rene, how much easier that is with white people than with us. Maybe because there are so many more of them, or maybe because they are secure and so don't have to bother. I've never quite decided."

Irene was inclined to be incredulous. "You mean that you didn't have to explain where you came from? It seems impossible."

Clare cast a glance of repressed amusement across the table at her. "As a matter of fact, I didn't. Though I suppose under any other circumstances I might have had to provide some plausible tale to account for myself. I've a good imagination, so I'm sure I could have done it quite creditably, and credibly. But it wasn't necessary. There were my aunts, you see, respectable and authentic enough for anything or anybody."

"I see. They were 'passing' too."

"No. They weren't. They were white."

"Oh!" And in the next instant it came back to Irene that she had heard this mentioned before; by her father, or, more likely, her mother. They were Bob Kendry's aunts. He had been a son of their brother's, on the left hand.[8] A wild oat.

"They were nice old ladies," Clare explained, "very religious and as poor as church mice. That adored brother of theirs, my grandfather, got through every penny they had after he'd finished his own little bit."

Clare paused in her narrative to light another cigarette. Her smile, her expression, Irene noticed, was faintly resentful.

"Being good Christians," she continued, "when dad came to his tipsy end, they did their duty and gave me a home of sorts. I was, it was true, expected to earn my keep by doing all the housework and most of the washing. But do you realize, 'Rene, that if it hadn't been for them, I shouldn't have had a home in the world?"

Irene's nod and little murmur were comprehensive, understanding.

Clare made a small mischievous grimace and proceeded. "Besides, to their notion, hard labour was good for me. I had Negro blood and they belonged to the generation that had written and read long articles headed: 'Will the Blacks Work?' Too, they weren't quite sure that the good God hadn't intended the sons and daughters of Ham[9] to sweat because he had poked fun at old man Noah once when he had taken a drop too much. I remember the aunts telling me that that old drunkard had cursed Ham and his sons for all time."

Irene laughed. But Clare remained quite serious.

"It was more than a joke, I assure you, 'Rene. It was a hard life for a girl of sixteen. Still, I had a roof over my head, and food, and clothes—such as they were. And there were the Scriptures, and talks on morals and thrift and industry and the loving-kindness of the good Lord."

"Have you ever stopped to think, Clare," Irene demanded, "how much unhappiness and downright cruelty are laid to the loving-kindness of the Lord? And always by His most ardent followers, it seems."

"Have I?" Clare exclaimed. "It, they, made me what I am today. For, of course, I was determined to get away, to be a person and not a charity or a problem, or even a daughter of the indiscreet Ham. Then, too, I wanted things. I knew I wasn't bad-looking and that I could 'pass.' You can't know, 'Rene, how, when I used to go over to the south side, I used almost to hate all of you. You had all the things I wanted and never had had. It made me all the more determined to get them, and others. Do you, can you understand what I felt?"

She looked up with a pointed and appealing effect, and, evidently finding the sympathetic expression on Irene's face sufficient answer, went on. "The aunts were queer. For all their Bibles and praying and ranting about honesty, they didn't want anyone to know that their darling brother had seduced—ruined, they called it—a Negro girl. They could excuse the ruin, but they couldn't forgive the tar-brush.[10] They forbade me to mention Negroes to the neighbours, or even to mention the south side. You may be sure that I didn't. I'll bet they were good and sorry afterwards."

She laughed and the ringing bells in her laugh had a hard metallic sound.

"When the chance to get away came, that omission was of great value to me. When Jack, a schoolboy acquaintance of some people in the neighbourhood, turned up from South America with untold gold, there was no one to tell him that I was coloured, and many to tell him about the severity and the religiousness of Aunt Grace and Aunt Edna. You can guess the rest. After he came, I stopped slipping off to the south side and slipped off to meet him instead. I couldn't manage both. In the end I had no great difficulty in convincing him that it was useless to talk marriage to the aunts. So on the day that I was eighteen, we went off and were married. So that's that. Nothing could have been easier."

"Yes, I do see that for you it was easy enough. By the way! I wonder why they didn't tell father that you were married. He went over to find out about you when you stopped coming over to see us. I'm sure they didn't tell him. Not that you were married."

Clare Kendry's eyes were bright with tears that didn't fall. "Oh, how lovely! To have cared enough about me to do that. The dear sweet man! Well, they couldn't tell him because they didn't know it. I took care of that, for I couldn't be sure that those consciences of theirs wouldn't begin to work on them afterwards and make them let the cat out of the bag. The old things probably thought I was living in sin, wherever I was. And it would be about what they expected."

An amused smile lit the lovely face for the smallest fraction of a second. After a little silence she said soberly: "But I'm sorry if they told your father so. That was something I hadn't counted on."

"I'm not sure that they did," Irene told her. "He didn't say so, anyway."

"He wouldn't, 'Rene dear. Not your father."

"Thanks. I'm sure he wouldn't."

"But you've never answered my question. Tell me, honestly, haven't you ever thought of 'passing'?"

Irene answered promptly: "No. Why should I?" And so disdainful was her voice and manner that Clare's face flushed and her eyes glinted. Irene hastened to add: "You see, Clare, I've everything I want. Except, perhaps, a little more money."

At that Clare laughed, her spark of anger vanished as quickly as it had appeared. "Of course," she declared, "that's what everybody wants, just a little more money, even the people who have it. And I must say I don't blame them. Money's awfully nice to have. In fact, all things considered, I think, 'Rene, that it's even worth the price."

Irene could only shrug her shoulders. Her reason partly agreed, her instinct wholly rebelled. And she could not say why. And though conscious that if she didn't hurry away, she was going to be late to dinner, she still lingered. It was as if the woman sitting on the other side of the table, a girl that she had known, who had done this rather dangerous and, to Irene Redfield, abhorrent thing successfully and had announced herself well satisfied, had for her a fascination, strange and compelling.

Clare Kendry was still leaning back in the tall chair, her sloping shoulders against the carved top. She sat with an air of indifferent assurance, as if arranged for, desired. About her clung that dim suggestion of polite insolence with which a few women are born and which some acquire with the coming of riches or importance.

Clare, it gave Irene a little prick of satisfaction to recall, hadn't got that by passing herself off as white. She herself had always had it.

Just as she'd always had that pale gold hair, which, unsheared still, was drawn loosely back from a broad brow,

partly hidden by the small close hat. Her lips, painted a brilliant geranium-red, were sweet and sensitive and a little ob-
stinate. A tempting mouth. The face across the forehead and
cheeks was a trifle too wide, but the ivory skin had a peculiar
soft lustre. And the eyes were magnificent! dark, sometimes
absolutely black, always luminous, and set in long, black
lashes. Arresting eyes, slow and mesmeric, and with, for all
their warmth, something withdrawn and secret about them.

Ah! Surely! They were Negro eyes! mysterious and concealing. And set in that ivory face under that bright hair, there was
about them something exotic.

Yes, Clare Kendry's loveliness was absolute, beyond challenge, thanks to those eyes which her grandmother and later
her mother and father had given her.

Into those eyes there came a smile and over Irene the sense
of being petted and caressed. She smiled back.

"Maybe," Clare suggested, "you can come Monday, if you're
back. Or, if you're not, then Tuesday."

With a small regretful sigh, Irene informed Clare that she
was afraid she wouldn't be back by Monday and that she was
sure she had dozens of things for Tuesday, and that she was
leaving Wednesday. It might be, however, that she could get
out of something Tuesday.

"Oh, do try. Do put somebody else off. The others can see
you any time, while I—Why, I may never see you again! Think
of that, 'Rene! You'll have to come. You'll simply have to! I'll
never forgive you if you don't."

At that moment it seemed a dreadful thing to think of never
seeing Clare Kendry again. Standing there under the appeal,
the caress, of her eyes, Irene had the desire, the hope, that this
parting wouldn't be the last.

"I'll try, Clare," she promised gently. "I'll call you—or will
you call me?"

"I think, perhaps, I'd better call you. Your father's in the
book, I know, and the address is the same. Sixty-four eighteen.
Some memory, what? Now remember, I'm going to expect
you. You've got to be able to come."

Again that peculiar mellowing smile.

"I'll do my best, Clare."

Irene gathered up her gloves and bag. They stood up. She put out her hand. Clare took and held it.

"It has been nice seeing you again, Clare. How pleased and glad father'll be to hear about you!"

"Until Tuesday, then," Clare Kendry replied. "I'll spend every minute of the time from now on looking forward to seeing you again. Good-bye, 'Rene dear. My love to your father, and this kiss for him."

The sun had gone from overhead, but the streets were still like fiery furnaces. The languid breeze was still hot. And the scurrying people looked even more wilted than before Irene had fled from their contact.

Crossing the avenue in the heat, far from the coolness of the Drayton's roof, away from the seduction of Clare Kendry's smile, she was aware of a sense of irritation with herself because she had been pleased and a little flattered at the other's obvious gladness at their meeting.

With her perspiring progress homeward this irritation grew, and she began to wonder just what had possessed her to make her promise to find time, in the crowded days that remained of her visit, to spend another afternoon with a woman whose life had so definitely and deliberately diverged from hers; and whom, as had been pointed out, she might never see again.

Why in the world had she made such a promise?

As she went up the steps to her father's house, thinking with what interest and amazement he would listen to her story of the afternoon's encounter, it came to her that Clare had omitted to mention her marriage name. She had referred to her husband as Jack. That was all. Had that, Irene asked herself, been intentional?

Clare had only to pick up the telephone to communicate with her, or to drop her a card, or to jump into a taxi. But she couldn't reach Clare in any way. Nor could anyone else to whom she might speak of their meeting.

"As if I should!"

Her key turned in the lock. She went in. Her father, it seemed, hadn't come in yet.

Irene decided that she wouldn't, after all, say anything to him about Clare Kendry. She had, she told herself, no inclination to speak of a person who held so low an opinion of her loyalty, or her discretion. And certainly she had no desire or intention of making the slightest effort about Tuesday. Nor any other day for that matter.

She was through with Clare Kendry.

THREE

On Tuesday morning a dome of grey sky rose over the parched city, but the stifling air was not relieved by the silvery mist that seemed to hold a promise of rain, which did not fall.

To Irene Redfield this soft foreboding fog was another reason for doing nothing about seeing Clare Kendry that afternoon.

But she did see her.

The telephone. For hours it had rung like something possessed. Since nine o'clock she had been hearing its insistent jangle. Awhile she was resolute, saying firmly each time: "Not in, Liza, take the message." And each time the servant returned with the information: "It's the same lady, ma'am; she says she'll call again."

But at noon, her nerves frayed and her conscience smiting her at the reproachful look on Liza's ebony face as she withdrew for another denial, Irene weakened.

"Oh, never mind. I'll answer this time, Liza."

"It's her again."

"Hello. . . . Yes."

"It's Clare, 'Rene. . . . Where *have* you been? . . . Can you be here around four? . . . What? . . . But, 'Rene, you promised! Just for a little while. . . . You can if you want to. . . . I am *so* disappointed. I had counted so on seeing you. . . . Please be nice and come. Only for a minute. I'm sure you can manage it if you try. . . . I won't beg you to stay. . . . Yes. . . . I'm going to expect you . . . It's the Morgan . . .[1] Oh, yes! The name's Bellew, Mrs. John Bellew. . . . About four, then. . . . I'll be so happy to see you! . . . Goodbye."

"Damn!"

Irene hung up the receiver with an emphatic bang, her thoughts immediately filled with self-reproach. She'd done it again. Allowed Clare Kendry to persuade her into promising to do something for which she had neither time nor any special desire. What was it about Clare's voice that was so appealing, so very seductive?

Clare met her in the hall with a kiss. She said: "You're good to come, 'Rene. But, then, you always were nice to me." And under her potent smile a part of Irene's annoyance with herself fled. She was even a little glad that she had come.

Clare led the way, stepping lightly, towards a room whose door was standing partly open, saying: "There's a surprise. It's a real party. See."

Entering, Irene found herself in a sitting-room, large and high, at whose windows hung startling blue draperies which triumphantly dragged attention from the gloomy chocolate-coloured furniture. And Clare was wearing a thin floating dress of the same shade of blue, which suited her and the rather difficult room to perfection.

For a minute Irene thought the room was empty, but turning her head, she discovered, sunk deep in the cushions of a huge sofa, a woman staring up at her with such intense concentration that her eyelids were drawn as though the strain of that upward glance had paralysed them. At first Irene took her to be a stranger, but in the next instant she said in an unsympathetic, almost harsh voice: "And how are you, Gertrude?"

The woman nodded and forced a smile to her pouting lips. "I'm all right," she replied. "And you're just the same, Irene. Not changed a bit."

"Thank you." Irene responded, as she chose a seat. She was thinking: "Great goodness! Two of them."

For Gertrude too had married a white man, though it couldn't be truthfully said that she was "passing." Her husband—what was his name?—had been in school with her and had been quite well aware, as had his family and most of his friends, that she was a Negro. It hadn't, Irene knew, seemed to matter to him then. Did it now, she wondered? Had Fred—Fred Martin, that was it—had he ever regretted his marriage because of Gertrude's race? Had Gertrude?

Turning to Gertrude, Irene asked: "And Fred, how is he? It's unmentionable years since I've seen him."

"Oh, he's all right," Gertrude answered briefly.

For a full minute no one spoke. Finally out of the oppressive little silence Clare's voice came pleasantly, conversationally: "We'll have tea right away. I know that you can't stay long, 'Rene. And I'm so sorry you won't see Margery. We went up the lake over the week end to see some of Jack's people, just out of Milwaukee. Margery wanted to stay with the children. It seemed a shame not to let her, especially since it's so hot in town. But I'm expecting Jack any second."

Irene said briefly: "That's nice."

Gertrude remained silent. She was, it was plain, a little ill at ease. And her presence there annoyed Irene, roused in her a defensive and resentful feeling for which she had at the moment no explanation. But it did seem to her odd that the woman that Clare was now should have invited the woman that Gertrude was. Still, of course, Clare couldn't have known. Twelve years since they had met.

Later, when she examined her feeling of annoyance, Irene admitted, a shade reluctantly, that it arose from a feeling of being outnumbered, a sense of aloneness, in her adherence to her own class and kind; not merely in the great thing of marriage, but in the whole pattern of her life as well.

Clare spoke again, this time at length. Her talk was of the change that Chicago presented to her after her long absence in European cities. Yes, she said in reply to some question from Gertrude, she'd been back to America a time or two, but only as far as New York and Philadelphia, and once she had spent a few days in Washington. John Bellew, who, it appeared, was some sort of international banking agent, hadn't particularly wanted her to come with him on this trip, but as soon as she had learned that it would probably take him as far as Chicago, she made up her mind to come anyway.

"I simply had to. And after I once got here, I was determined

to see someone I knew and find out what had happened to
everybody. I didn't quite see how I was going to manage it, but
I meant to. Somehow. I'd just about decided to take a chance
and go out to your house, 'Rene, or call up and arrange a
meeting, when I ran into you. What luck!"

Irene agreed that it was luck. "It's the first time I've been
home for five years, and now I'm about to leave. A week later
and I'd have been gone. And how in the world did you find
Gertrude?"

"In the book. I remembered about Fred. His father still has
the meat market."

"Oh, yes," said Irene, who had only remembered it as Clare
had spoken, "on Cottage Grove[2] near—"

Gertrude broke in. "No. It's moved. We're on Maryland
Avenue—used to be Jackson—now. Near Sixty-third Street.[3]
And the market's Fred's. His name's the same as his father's."

Gertrude, Irene thought, looked as if her husband might be
a butcher. There was left of her youthful prettiness, which had
been so much admired in their high-school days, no trace. She
had grown broad, fat almost, and though there were no lines
on her large white face, its very smoothness was somehow
prematurely ageing. Her black hair was clipt, and by some
unfortunate means all the live curliness had gone from it. Her
over-trimmed Georgette *crêpe* dress was too short and showed
an appalling amount of leg, stout legs in sleazy stockings of a
vivid rose-beige shade. Her plump hands were newly and not
too competently manicured—for the occasion, probably. And
she wasn't smoking.

Clare said—and Irene fancied that her husky voice held a
slight edge—"Before you came, Irene, Gertrude was telling
me about her two boys. Twins. Think of it! Isn't it too marvellous for words?"

Irene felt a warmness creeping into her cheeks. Uncanny,
the way Clare could divine what one was thinking. She was a
little put out, but her manner was entirely easy as she said:
"That is nice. I've two boys myself, Gertrude. Not twins,
though. It seems that Clare's rather behind, doesn't it?"

Gertrude, however, wasn't sure that Clare hadn't the best of it. "She's got a girl. I wanted a girl. So did Fred."

"Isn't that a bit unusual?" Irene asked. "Most men want sons. Egotism, I suppose."

"Well, Fred didn't."

The tea-things had been placed on a low table at Clare's side. She gave them her attention now, pouring the rich amber fluid from the tall glass pitcher into stately slim glasses, which she handed to her guests, and then offered them lemon or cream and tiny sandwiches or cakes.

After taking up her own glass she informed them: "No, I have no boys and I don't think I'll ever have any. I'm afraid. I nearly died of terror the whole nine months before Margery was born for fear that she might be dark. Thank goodness, she turned out all right. But I'll never risk it again. Never! The strain is simply too—too hellish."

Gertrude Martin nodded in complete comprehension.

This time it was Irene who said nothing.

"You don't have to tell me!" Gertrude said fervently. "I know what it is all right. Maybe you don't think I wasn't scared to death too. Fred said I was silly, and so did his mother. But, of course, they thought it was just a notion I'd gotten into my head and they blamed it on my condition. They don't know like we do, how it might go way back, and turn out dark no matter what colour the father and mother are."

Perspiration stood out on her forehead. Her narrow eyes rolled first in Clare's, then in Irene's direction. As she talked she waved her heavy hands about.

"No," she went on, "no more for me either. Not even a girl. It's awful the way it skips generations and then pops out. Why, he actually said he didn't care what colour it turned out, if I would only stop worrying about it. But, of course, nobody wants a dark child." Her voice was earnest and she took for granted that her audience was in entire agreement with her.

Irene, whose head had gone up with a quick little jerk, now said in a voice of whose even tones she was proud: "One of my boys is dark."

Gertrude jumped as if she had been shot at. Her eyes goggled. Her mouth flew open. She tried to speak, but could not immediately get the words out. Finally she managed to stammer: "Oh! And your husband, is he—is he—er—dark, too?"

Irene, who was struggling with a flood of feelings, resentment, anger, and contempt, was, however, still able to answer as coolly as if she had not that sense of not belonging to and of despising the company in which she found herself drinking iced tea from tall amber glasses on that hot August afternoon. Her husband, she informed them quietly, couldn't exactly "pass."

At that reply Clare turned on Irene her seductive caressing smile and remarked a little scoffingly: "I do think that coloured people—we—are too silly about some things. After all, the thing's not important to Irene or hundreds of others. Not awfully, even to you, Gertrude. It's only deserters like me who have to be afraid of freaks of the nature. As my inestimable dad used to say, 'Everything must be paid for.' Now, please one of you tell me what ever happened to Claude Jones. You know, the tall, lanky specimen who used to wear that comical little moustache that the girls used to laugh at so. Like a thin streak of soot. The moustache, I mean."

At that Gertrude shrieked with laughter. "Claude Jones!" and launched into the story of how he was no longer a Negro or a Christian but had become a Jew.

"A Jew!" Clare exclaimed.

"Yes, a Jew. A black Jew, he calls himself. He won't eat ham and goes to the synagogue on Saturday. He's got a beard now as well as a moustache. You'd die laughing if you saw him. He's really too funny for words. Fred says he's crazy and I guess he is. Oh, he's a scream all right, a regular scream!" And she shrieked again.

Clare's laugh tinkled out. "It certainly sounds funny enough. Still, it's his own business. If he gets along better by turning—"

At that, Irene, who was still hugging her unhappy don't-care feeling of rightness, broke in, saying bitingly: "It evidently doesn't occur to either you or Gertrude that he might possibly be sincere in changing his religion. Surely everyone doesn't do everything for gain."

Clare Kendry had no need to search for the full meaning of that utterance. She reddened slightly and retorted seriously: "Yes, I admit that might be possible—his being sincere, I mean. It just didn't happen to occur to me, that's all. I'm surprised," and the seriousness changed to mockery, "that you should have expected it to. Or did you really?"

"You don't, I'm sure, imagine that that is a question that I can answer," Irene told her. "Not here and now."

Gertrude's face expressed complete bewilderment. However, seeing that little smiles had come out on the faces of the two other women and not recognizing them for the smiles of mutual reservations which they were, she smiled too.

Clare began to talk, steering carefully away from anything that might lead towards race or other thorny subjects. It was the most brilliant exhibition of conversational weightlifting that Irene had ever seen. Her words swept over them in charming well-modulated streams. Her laughs tinkled and pealed. Her little stories sparkled.

Irene contributed a bare "Yes" or "No" here and there. Gertrude, a "You don't say!" less frequently.

For a while the illusion of general conversation was nearly perfect. Irene felt her resentment changing gradually to a silent, somewhat grudging admiration.

Clare talked on, her voice, her gestures colouring all she said of wartime in France, of after-the-wartime in Germany, of the excitement at the time of the general strike in England, of dressmaker's openings in Paris, of the new gaiety of Budapest.[4]

But it couldn't last, this verbal feat. Gertrude shifted in her seat and fell to fidgeting with her fingers. Irene, bored at last by all this repetition of the selfsame things that she had read all too often in papers, magazines, and books, set down her glass and collected her bag and handkerchief. She was smoothing out the tan fingers of her gloves preparatory to putting them on when she heard the sound of the outer door being opened and saw Clare spring up with an expression of relief saying: "How lovely! Here's Jack at exactly the right minute. You can't go now, 'Rene dear."

John Bellew came into the room. The first thing that Irene noticed about him was that he was not the man that she had seen with Clare Kendry on the Drayton roof. This man, Clare's husband, was a tallish person, broadly made. His age she guessed to be somewhere between thirty-five and forty. His hair was dark brown and waving, and he had a soft mouth, somewhat womanish, set in an unhealthy-looking dough-coloured face. His steel-grey opaque eyes were very much alive, moving ceaselessly between thick bluish lids. But there was, Irene decided, nothing unusual about him, unless it was an impression of latent physical power.

"Hello, Nig," was his greeting to Clare.

Gertrude who had started slightly, settled back and looked covertly towards Irene, who had caught her lip between her teeth and sat gazing at husband and wife. It was hard to believe that even Clare Kendry would permit this ridiculing of her race by an outsider, though he chanced to be her husband. So he knew, then, that Clare was a Negro? From her talk the other day Irene had understood that he didn't. But how rude, how positively insulting, for him to address her in that way in the presence of guests!

In Clare's eyes, as she presented her husband, was a queer gleam, a jeer, it might be. Irene couldn't define it.

The mechanical professions that attend an introduction over, she inquired: "Did you hear what Jack called me?"

"Yes," Gertrude answered, laughing with a dutiful eagerness.

Irene didn't speak. Her gaze remained level on Clare's smiling face.

The black eyes fluttered down. "Tell them, dear, why you call me that."

The man chuckled, crinkling up his eyes, not, Irene was compelled to acknowledge, unpleasantly. He explained: "Well, you see, it's like this. When we were first married, she was as white as—as—well as white as a lily. But I declare she's gettin' darker and darker. I tell her if she don't look out, she'll wake up one of these days and find she's turned into a nigger."

He roared with laughter. Clare's ringing bell-like laugh

joined his. Gertrude after another uneasy shift in her seat added
her shrill one. Irene, who had been sitting with lips tightly
compressed, cried out: "That's good!" and gave way to gales
of laughter. She laughed and laughed and laughed. Tears ran
down her cheeks. Her sides ached. Her throat hurt. She laughed
on and on and on, long after the others had subsided. Until,
catching sight of Clare's face, the need for a more quiet enjoy-
ment of this priceless joke, and for caution, struck her. At once
she stopped.

Clare handed her husband his tea and laid her hand on his
arm with an affectionate little gesture. Speaking with confidence as well as with amusement, she said: "My goodness,
Jack! What difference would it make if, after all these years,
you were to find out that I was one or two per cent coloured?"

Bellew put out his hand in a repudiating fling, definite and
final. "Oh, no, Nig," he declared, "nothing like that with me.
I know you're no nigger, so it's all right. You can get as black
as you please as far as I'm concerned, since I know you're no
nigger. I draw the line at that. No niggers in my family. Never
have been and never will be."

Irene's lips trembled almost uncontrollably, but she made a
desperate effort to fight back her disastrous desire to laugh
again, and succeeded. Carefully selecting a cigarette from the
lacquered box on the tea-table before her, she turned an oblique
look on Clare and encountered her peculiar eyes fixed on her
with an expression so dark and deep and unfathomable that
she had for a short moment the sensation of gazing into the
eyes of some creature utterly strange and apart. A faint sense
of danger brushed her, like the breath of a cold fog. Absurd,
her reason told her, as she accepted Bellew's proffered light for
her cigarette. Another glance at Clare showed her smiling. So,
as one always ready to oblige, was Gertrude.

An on-looker, Irene reflected, would have thought it a most
congenial tea-party, all smiles and jokes and hilarious laughter.
She said humorously: "So you dislike Negroes, Mr. Bellew?"
But her amusement was at her thought, rather than her words.

John Bellew gave a short denying laugh. "You got me wrong
there, Mrs. Redfield. Nothing like that at all. I don't dislike

them, I hate them. And so does Nig, for all she's trying to turn into one. She wouldn't have a nigger maid around her for love nor money. Not that I'd want her to. They give me the creeps. The black scrimy devils."

This wasn't funny. Had Bellew, Irene inquired, ever known any Negroes? The defensive tone of her voice brought another start from the uncomfortable Gertrude, and, for all her appearance of serenity, a quick apprehensive look from Clare.

Bellew answered: "Thank the Lord, no! And never expect to! But I know people who've known them, better than they know their black selves. And I read in the papers about them. Always robbing and killing people. And," he added darkly, "worse."

From Gertrude's direction came a queer little suppressed sound, a snort or a giggle. Irene couldn't tell which. There was a brief silence, during which she feared that her self control was about to prove too frail a bridge to support her mounting anger and indignation. She had a leaping desire to shout at the man beside her: "And you're sitting here surrounded by three black devils, drinking tea."

The impulse passed, obliterated by her consciousness of the danger in which such rashness would involve Clare, who remarked with a gentle reprovingness: "Jack dear, I'm sure 'Rene doesn't care to hear all about your pet aversions. Nor Gertrude either. Maybe they read the papers too, you know." She smiled on him, and her smile seemed to transform him, to soften and mellow him, as the rays of the sun does a fruit.

"All right, Nig, old girl. I'm sorry," he apologized. Reaching over, he playfully touched his wife's pale hands, then turned back to Irene. "Didn't mean to bore you, Mrs. Redfield. Hope you'll excuse me," he said sheepishly. "Clare tells me you're living in New York. Great city, New York. The city of the future."

In Irene, rage had not retreated, but was held by some dam of caution and allegiance to Clare. So, in the best casual voice she could muster, she agreed with Bellew. Though, she reminded him, it was exactly what Chicagoans were apt to say of their city. And all the while she was speaking, she was thinking how amazing it was that her voice did not tremble, that outwardly she was calm. Only her hands shook slightly. She drew them inward from their rest in her lap and pressed the tips of her fingers together to still them.

"Husband's a doctor, I understand. Manhattan, or one of the other boroughs?"

Manhattan, Irene informed him, and explained the need for Brian to be within easy reach of certain hospitals and clinics.

"Interesting life, a doctor's."

"Ye-es. Hard, though. And, in a way, monotonous. Nerve-racking too."

"Hard on the wife's nerves at least, eh? So many lady patients." He laughed, enjoying, with a boyish heartiness, the hoary joke.

Irene managed a momentary smile, but her voice was sober as she said: "Brian doesn't care for ladies, especially sick ones. I sometimes wish he did. It's South America that attracts him."

"Coming place, South America, if they ever get the niggers out of it. It's run over—"

"Really, Jack!" Clare's voice was on the edge of temper.

"Honestly, Nig, I forgot." To the others he said: "You see how hen-pecked I am." And to Gertrude: "You're still in Chicago, Mrs.—er—Mrs. Martin?"

He was, it was plain, doing his best to be agreeable to these old friends of Clare's. Irene had to concede that under other conditions she might have liked him. A fairly good-looking man of amiable disposition, evidently, and in easy circumstances. Plain and with no nonsense about him.

Gertrude replied that Chicago was good enough for her. She'd never been out of it and didn't think she ever should. Her husband's business was there.

"Of course, of course. Can't jump up and leave a business."

There followed a smooth surface of talk about Chicago, New York, their differences and their recent spectacular changes.

It was, Irene, thought, unbelievable and astonishing that four people could sit so unruffled, so ostensibly friendly, while they were in reality seething with anger, mortification, shame. But no, on second thought she was forced to amend her opinion. John Bellew, most certainly, was as undisturbed within as without. So, perhaps, was Gertrude Martin. At least she hadn't the mortification and shame that Clare Kendry must be feeling, or, in such full measure, the rage and rebellion that she, Irene, was repressing.

"More tea, 'Rene," Clare offered.

"Thanks, no. And I must be going. I'm leaving tomorrow, you know, and I've still got packing to do."

She stood up. So did Gertrude, and Clare, and John Bellew.

"How do you like the Drayton, Mrs. Redfield?" the latter asked.

"The Drayton? Oh, very much. Very much indeed," Irene answered, her scornful eyes on Clare's unrevealing face.

"Nice place, all right. Stayed there a time or two myself," the man informed her.

"Yes, it is nice," Irene agreed. "Almost as good as our best New York places." She had withdrawn her look from Clare and was searching in her bag for some non-existent something. Her understanding was rapidly increasing, as was her pity and her contempt. Clare was so daring, so lovely, and so "having."

They gave their hands to Clare with appropriate murmurs. "So good to have seen you." . . . "I do hope I'll see you again soon."

"Good-bye," Clare returned. "It was good of you to come, 'Rene dear. And you too, Gertrude."

"Good-bye, Mr. Bellew." . . . "So glad to have met you." It was Gertrude who had said that. Irene couldn't, she absolutely couldn't bring herself to utter the polite fiction or anything approaching it.

He accompanied them out into the hall, summoned the elevator.

"Good-bye," they said again, stepping in.

Plunging downward they were silent.

They made their way through the lobby without speaking.

But as soon as they had reached the street Gertrude, in the manner of one unable to keep bottled up for another minute

that which for the last hour she had had to retain, burst out:
"My God! What an awful chance! She must be plumb crazy."

"Yes, it certainly seems risky," Irene admitted.

"Risky! I should say it was. Risky! My God! What a word!
And the mess she's liable to get herself into!"

"Still, I imagine she's pretty safe. They don't live here, you
know. And there's a child. That's a certain security."

"It's an awful chance, just the same," Gertrude insisted. "I'd
never in the world have married Fred without him knowing.
You can't tell what will turn up."

"Yes, I do agree that it's safer to tell. But then Bellew wouldn't
have married her. And, after all, that's what she wanted."

Gertrude shook her head. "I wouldn't be in her shoes for
all the money she's getting out of it, when he finds out. Not
with him feeling the way he does. Gee! Wasn't it awful? For
a minute I was so mad I could have slapped him."

It had been, Irene acknowledged, a distinctly trying experience, as well as a very unpleasant one. "I was more than a
little angry myself."

"And imagine her not telling us about him feeling that way!
Anything might have happened. We might have said something."

That, Irene pointed out, was exactly like Clare Kendry. Taking a chance, and not at all considering anyone else's feelings.

Gertrude said: "Maybe she thought we'd think it a good
joke. And I guess you did. The way you laughed. My land! I
was scared to death he might catch on."

"Well, it was rather a joke," Irene told her, "on him and us
and maybe on her."

"All the same, it's an awful chance. I'd hate to be her."

"She seems satisfied enough. She's got what she wanted, and
the other day she told me it was worth it."

But about that Gertrude was sceptical. "She'll find out different," was her verdict. "She'll find out different all right."

Rain had begun to fall, a few scattered large drops.

The end-of-the-day crowds were scurrying in the directions
of street-cars and elevated roads.

Irene said: "You're going south? I'm sorry. I've got an errand.

If you don't mind, I'll just say good-bye here. It has been nice seeing you, Gertrude. Say hello to Fred for me, and to your mother if she remembers me. Good-bye."

She had wanted to be free of the other woman, to be alone; for she was still sore and angry.

What right, she kept demanding of herself, had Clare Kendry to expose her, or even Gertrude Martin, to such humiliation, such downright insult?

And all the while, on the rushing ride out to her father's house, Irene Redfield was trying to understand the look on Clare's face as she had said good-bye. Partly mocking, it had seemed, and partly menacing. And something else for which she could find no name. For an instant a recrudescence of that sensation of fear which she had had while looking into Clare's eyes that afternoon touched her. A slight shiver ran over her.

"It's nothing," she told herself. "Just somebody walking over my grave, as the children say." She tried a tiny laugh and was annoyed to find that it was close to tears.

What a state she had allowed that horrible Bellew to get her into!

And late that night, even, long after the last guest had gone and the old house was quiet, she stood at her window frowning out into the dark rain and puzzling again over that look on Clare's incredibly beautiful face. She couldn't, however, come to any conclusion about its meaning, try as she might. It was unfathomable, utterly beyond any experience or comprehension of hers.

She turned away from the window, at last, with a still deeper frown. Why, after all, worry about Clare Kendry? She was well able to take care of herself, had always been able. And there were, for Irene, other things, more personal and more important to worry about.

Besides, her reason told her, she had only herself to blame for her disagreeable afternoon and its attendant fears and questions. She ought never to have gone.

FOUR

The next morning, the day of her departure for New York, had brought a letter, which, at first glance, she had instinctively known came from Clare Kendry, though she couldn't remember ever having had a letter from her before. Ripping it open and looking at the signature, she saw that she had been right in her guess. She wouldn't, she told herself, read it. She hadn't the time. And, besides, she had no wish to be reminded of the afternoon before. As it was, she felt none too fresh for her journey; she had had a wretched night. And all because of Clare's innate lack of consideration for the feelings of others.

But she did read it. After father and friends had waved goodbye, and she was being hurled eastward, she became possessed of an uncontrollable curiosity to see what Clare had said about yesterday. For what, she asked, as she took it out of her bag and opened it, could she, what could anyone, say about a thing like that?

Clare Kendry had said:

'Rene dear:

However am I to thank you for your visit? I know you are feeling that under the circumstances I ought not to have asked you to come, or, rather, insisted. But if you could know how glad, how excitingly happy, I was to meet you and how I ached to see more of you (to see everybody and couldn't), you would understand my wanting to see you again, and maybe forgive me a little.

My love to you always and always and to your dear father, and all my poor thanks.

CLARE.

And there was a postscript which said:

It may be, 'Rene dear, it may just be, that, after all, your way may be the wiser and infinitely happier one. I'm not sure just now. At least not so sure as I have been.

C.

But the letter hadn't conciliated Irene. Her indignation was not lessened by Clare's flattering reference to her wiseness. As if, she thought wrathfully, anything could take away the humiliation, or any part of it, of what she had gone through yesterday afternoon for Clare Kendry.

With an unusual methodicalness she tore the offending letter into tiny ragged squares that fluttered down and made a small heap in her black *crêpe de Chine* lap. The destruction completed, she gathered them up, rose, and moved to the train's end. Standing there, she dropped them over the railing and watched them scatter, on tracks, on cinders, on forlorn grass, in rills of dirty water.

And that, she told herself, was that. The chances were one in a million that she would ever again lay eyes on Clare Kendry. If, however, that millionth chance should turn up, she had only to turn away her eyes, to refuse her recognition.

She dropped Clare out of her mind and turned her thoughts to her own affairs. To home, to the boys, to Brian. Brian, who in the morning would be waiting for her in the great clamourous station. She hoped that he had been comfortable and not too lonely without her and the boys. Not so lonely that that old, queer, unhappy restlessness had begun again within him, that craving for some place strange and different, which at the beginning of her marriage she had had to make such strenuous efforts to repress, and which yet faintly alarmed her, though it now sprang up at gradually lessening intervals.

PART TWO

RE-ENCOUNTER

ONE

Such were Irene Redfield's memories as she sat there in her room, a flood of October sunlight streaming in upon her, holding that second letter of Clare Kendry's.

Laying it aside, she regarded with an astonishment that had in it a mild degree of amusement the violence of the feelings which it stirred in her.

It wasn't the great measure of anger that surprised and slightly amused her. That, she was certain, was justified and reasonable, as was the fact that it could hold, still strong and unabated, across the stretch of two years' time entirely removed from any sight or sound of John Bellew, or of Clare. That even at this remote date the memory of the man's words and manner had power to set her hands to trembling and to send the blood pounding against her temples did not seem to her extraordinary. But that she should retain that dim sense of fear, of panic, was surprising, silly.

That Clare should have written, should even all things considered, have expressed a desire to see her again, did not so much amaze her. To count as nothing the annoyances, the bitterness, or the suffering of others, that was Clare.

Well—Irene's shoulders went up—one thing was sure: that she needn't, and didn't intend to, lay herself open to any repetition of a humiliation as galling and outrageous as that which, for Clare Kendry's sake, she had borne "that time in Chicago." Once was enough.

If, at the time of choosing, Clare hadn't precisely reckoned the cost, she had, nevertheless, no right to expect others to help make up the reckoning. The trouble with Clare was, not only that she wanted to have her cake and eat it too, but that she wanted to nibble at the cakes of other folk as well.

Irene Redfield found it hard to sympathize with this new tenderness, this avowed yearning of Clare's for "my own people."

The letter which she just put out of her hand was, to her taste, a bit too lavish in its wordiness, a shade too unreserved in the manner of its expression. It roused again that old suspicion that Clare was acting, not consciously, perhaps—that is, not too consciously—but, none the less, acting. Nor was Irene inclined to excuse what she termed Clare's downright selfishness.

And mingled with her disbelief and resentment was another feeling, a question. Why hadn't she spoken that day? Why, in the face of Bellew's ignorant hate and aversion, had she concealed her own origin? Why had she allowed him to make his assertions and express his misconceptions undisputed? Why simply because of Clare Kendry, who had exposed her to such torment, had she failed to take up the defence of the race to which she belonged?

Irene asked these questions, felt them. They were, however, merely rhetorical, as she herself was well aware. She knew their answers, every one, and it was the same for them all. The sardony of it![1] She couldn't betray Clare, couldn't even run the risk of appearing to defend a people that were being maligned, for fear that that defence might in some infinitesimal degree lead the way to final discovery of her secret. She had to Clare Kendry a duty. She was bound to her by those very ties of race, which, for all her repudiation of them, Clare had been unable to completely sever.

And it wasn't, as Irene knew, that Clare cared at all about the race or what was to become of it. She didn't. Or that she had for any of its members great, or even real, affection, though she professed undying gratitude for the small kindnesses which the Westover family had shown her when she was a child. Irene doubted the genuineness of it, seeing herself only as a means to an end where Clare was concerned. Nor could it be said that she had even the slight artistic or sociological interest in the race that some members of other races displayed. She hadn't. No, Clare Kendry cared nothing for the race. She only belonged to it.

"Not another damned thing!" Irene declared aloud as she drew a fragile stocking over a pale beige-coloured foot.

"Aha! Swearing again, are you, madam? Caught you in the act that time."

Brian Redfield had come into the room in that noiseless way which, in spite, of the years of their life together, still had the power to disconcert her. He stood looking down on her with that amused smile of his, which was just the faintest bit supercilious and yet was somehow very becoming to him.

Hastily Irene pulled on the other stocking and slipped her feet into the slippers beside her chair.

"And what brought on this particular outburst of profanity? That is, if an indulgent but perturbed husband may inquire. The mother of sons too! The times, alas, the times!"

"I've had this letter," Irene told him. "And I'm sure that anybody'll admit it's enough to make a saint swear. The nerve of her!"

She passed the letter to him, and in the act made a little mental frown. For, with a nicety of perception, she saw that she was doing it instead of answering his question with words, so that he might be occupied while she hurried through her dressing. For she was late again, and Brian, she well knew, detested that. Why, oh why, couldn't she ever manage to be on time? Brian had been up for ages, had made some calls for all she knew, besides having taken the boys downtown to school. And she wasn't dressed yet; had only begun. Damn Clare! This morning it was her fault.

Brian sat down and bent his head over the letter, puckering his brows slightly in his effort to make out Clare's scrawl.

Irene, who had risen and was standing before the mirror, ran a comb through her black hair, then tossed her head with a light characteristic gesture, in order to disarrange a little the set locks. She touched a powder-puff to her warm olive skin, and then put on her frock with a motion so hasty that it was with some difficulty properly adjusted. At last she was ready, though she didn't immediately say so, but stood, instead, looking with a sort of curious detachment at her husband across the room.

Brian, she was thinking, was extremely good-looking. Not, of course, pretty or effeminate; the slight irregularity of his nose saved him from the prettiness, and the rather marked heaviness of his chin saved him from the effeminacy. But he was, in a pleasant masculine way, rather handsome. And yet, wouldn't he, perhaps, have been merely ordinarily good-looking but for the richness, the beauty of his skin, which was of an exquisitely fine texture and deep copper colour.

He looked up and said: "Clare? That must be the girl you told me about meeting the last time you were out home. The one you went to tea with?"

Irene's answer to that was an inclination of the head.

"I'm ready," she said.

They were going downstairs, Brian deftly, unnecessarily, piloting her round the two short curved steps, just before the centre landing.

"You're not," he asked, "going to see her?"

His words, however, were in reality not a question, but, as Irene was aware, an admonition.

Her front teeth just touched. She spoke through them, and her tones held a thin sarcasm. "Brian, darling, I'm really not such an idiot that I don't realize that if a man calls me a nigger, it's his fault the first time, but mine if he has the opportunity to do it again."

They went into the dining-room. He drew back her chair and she sat down behind the fat-bellied German coffee-pot, which sent out its morning fragrance, mingled with the smell of crisp toast and savoury bacon, in the distance. With his long, nervous fingers he picked up the morning paper from his own chair and sat down.

Zulena, a small mahogany-coloured creature, brought in the grapefruit.

They took up their spoons.

Out of the silence Brian spoke. Blandly. "My dear, you misunderstand me entirely. I simply meant that I hope you're not going to let her pester you. She will, you know, if you give her half a chance and she's anything at all like your description of her. Anyway, they always do. Besides," he corrected, "the man, her husband, didn't call you a nigger. There's a difference, you know."

"No, certainly he didn't. Not actually. He couldn't, not very well, since he didn't know. But he would have. It amounts to the same thing. And I'm sure it was just as unpleasant."

"U-mm, I don't know. But it seems to me," he pointed out, "that you, my dear, had all the advantage. You knew what his opinion of you was, while he— Well, 'twas ever thus. We know, always have. They don't. Not quite. It has, you will admit, its humorous side, and, sometimes, its conveniences."

She poured the coffee.

"I can't see it. I'm going to write Clare. Today, if I can find a minute. It's a thing we might as well settle definitely, and immediately. Curious, isn't it, that knowing, as she does, his unqualified attitude, she still—"

Brian interrupted: "It's always that way. Never known it to fail. Remember Albert Hammond, how he used to be for ever haunting Seventh Avenue, and Lenox Avenue, and the dancing-places, until some 'shine' took a shot at him for casting an eye towards his 'sheba?'[2] They always come back. I've seen it happen time and time again."

"But why?" Irene wanted to know. "Why?"

"If I knew that, I'd know what race is."

"But wouldn't you think that having got the thing, or things, they were after, and at such risk, they'd be satisfied? Or afraid?"

"Yes," Brian agreed, "you certainly would think so. But, the fact remains, they aren't. Not satisfied, I mean. I think they're scared enough most of the time, when they give way to the urge and slip back. Not scared enough to stop them, though. Why, the good God only knows."

Irene leaned forward, speaking, she was aware, with a vehemence absolutely unnecessary, but which she could not control.

"Well, Clare can just count me out. I've no intention of being the link between her and her poorer darker brethren. After that scene in Chicago too! To calmly expect me—" She stopped short, suddenly too wrathful for words.

"Quite right. The only sensible thing to do. Let her miss you. It's an unhealthy business, the whole affair. Always is."

Irene nodded. "More coffee," she offered.

"Thanks, no." He took up his paper again, spreading it open with a little rattling noise.

Zulena came in bringing more toast. Brian took a slice and bit into it with that audible crunching sound that Irene disliked so intensely, and turned back to his paper.

She said: "It's funny about 'passing.' We disapprove of it and at the same time condone it. It excites our contempt and yet we rather admire it. We shy away from it with an odd kind of revulsion, but we protect it."

"Instinct of the race to survive and expand."

"Rot! Everything can't be explained by some general biological phrase."

"Absolutely everything can. Look at the so-called whites, who've left bastards all over the known earth. Same thing in them. Instinct of the race to survive and expand."

With that Irene didn't at all agree, but many arguments in the past had taught her the futility of attempting to combat Brian on ground where he was more nearly at home than she. Ignoring his unqualified assertion, she slid away from the subject entirely.

"I wonder," she asked, "if you'll have time to run me down to the printing-office. It's on a Hundred and Sixteenth Street. I've got to see about some handbills and some more tickets for the dance."

"Yes, of course. How's it going? Everything all set?"

"Ye-es. I guess so. The boxes are all sold and nearly all the first batch of tickets. And we expect to take in almost as much again at the door. Then, there's all that cake to sell. It's a terrible lot of work, though."

"I'll bet it is. Uplifting the brother's no easy job.[3] I'm as busy as a cat with fleas, myself." And over his face there came a shadow. "Lord! how I hate sick people, and their stupid,

meddling families, and smelly, dirty rooms, and climbing filthy
steps in dark hallways."

"Surely," Irene began, fighting back the fear and irritation
that she felt, "surely—"

Her husband silenced her, saying sharply: "Let's not talk
about it, please." And immediately, in his usual, slightly mocking tone he asked: "Are you ready to go now? I haven't a great
deal of time to wait."

He got up. She followed him out into the hall without reply-
ing. He picked up his soft brown hat from the small table and
stood a moment whirling it round on his long tea-coloured
fingers.

Irene, watching him, was thinking: "It isn't fair, it isn't fair."
After all these years to still blame her like this. Hadn't his success proved that she'd been right in insisting that he stick to
his profession right there in New York? Couldn't he see, even
now, that it *had* been best? Not for her, oh no, not for her—
she had never really considered herself—but for him and the
boys. Was she never to be free of it, that fear which crouched,
always, deep down within her, stealing away the sense of security, the feeling of permanence, from the life which she had
so admirably arranged for them all, and desired so ardently
to have remain as it was? That strange, and to her fantastic,
notion of Brian's of going off to Brazil, which, though unmen-
tioned, yet lived within him; how it frightened her, and—yes,
angered her!

"Well?" he asked lightly.

"I'll just get my things. One minute," she promised and
turned upstairs.

Her voice had been even and her step was firm, but in her
there was no slackening of the agitation, of the alarms, which
Brian's expression of discontent had raised. He had never spoken of his desire since that long-ago time of storm and strain,
of hateful and nearly disastrous quarrelling, when she had so
firmly opposed him, so sensibly pointed out its utter impossibility and its probable consequences to her and the boys, and
had even hinted at a dissolution of their marriage in the event
of his persistence in his idea. No, there had been, in all the

years that they had lived together since then, no other talk of it, no more than there had been any other quarrelling or any other threats. But because, so she insisted, the bond of flesh and spirit between them was so strong, she knew, had always known, that his dissatisfaction had continued, as had his dislike and disgust for his profession and his country.

A feeling of uneasiness stole upon her at the inconceivable suspicion that she might have been wrong in her estimate of her husband's character. But she squirmed away from it. Impossible! She couldn't have been wrong. Everything proved that she had been right. More than right, if such a thing could be. And all, she assured herself, because she understood him so well, because she had, actually, a special talent for understanding him. It was, as she saw it, the one thing that had been the basis of the success which she had made of a marriage that had threatened to fail. She knew him as well as he knew himself, or better.

Then why worry? The thing, this discontent which had exploded into words, would surely die, flicker out, at last. True, she had in the past often been tempted to believe that it had died, only to become conscious, in some instinctive, subtle way, that she had been merely deceiving herself for a while and that it still lived. But it *would* die. Of that she was certain. She had only to direct and guide her man, to keep him going in the right direction.

She put on her coat and adjusted her hat.

Yes, it would die, as long ago she had made up her mind that it should. But in the meantime, while it was still living and still had the power to flare up and alarm her, it would have to be banked, smothered, and something offered in its stead. She would have to make some plan, some decision, at once. She frowned, for it annoyed her intensely. For, though temporary, it would be important and perhaps disturbing. Irene didn't like changes, particularly changes that affected the smooth routine of her household. Well, it couldn't be helped. Something would have to be done. And immediately.

She took up her purse and drawing on her gloves, ran down

the steps and out through the door which Brian held open for her and stepped into the waiting car.

"You know," she said, settling herself into the seat beside him, "I'm awfuly glad to get this minute alone with you. It does seem that we're always so busy—I do hate that—but what can we do? I've had something on my mind for ever so long, something that needs talking over and really serious consideration."

The car's engine rumbled as it moved out from the kerb and into the scant traffic of the street under Brian's expert guidance.

She studied his profile.

They turned into Seventh Avenue. Then he said: "Well, let's have it. No time like the present for the settling of weighty matters."

"It's about Junior. I wonder if he isn't going too fast in school? We do forget that he's not eleven yet. Surely it can't be good for him to—well, if he is, I mean. Going too fast, you know. Of course, you know more about these things than I do. You're better able to judge. That is, if you've noticed or thought about it at all."

"I do wish, Irene, you wouldn't be for ever fretting about those kids. They're all right. Perfectly all right. Good, strong, healthy boys, especially Junior. Most especially Junior."

"We-ll, I s'pose you're right. You're expected to know about things like that, and I'm sure you wouldn't make a mistake about your own boy." (Now, why had she said that?) "But that isn't all. I'm terribly afraid he's picked up some queer ideas about things—some things—from the older boys, you know."

Her manner was consciously light. Apparently she was intent of the maze of traffic, but she was still watching Brian's face closely. On it was a peculiar expression. Was it, could it possibly be, a mixture of scorn and distaste?

"Queer ideas?" he repeated. "D'you mean ideas about sex, Irene?"

"Ye-es. Not quite nice ones. Dreadful jokes, and things like that."

"Oh, I see," he threw at her. For a while there was silence between them. After a moment he demanded bluntly: "Well, what of it? If sex isn't a joke, what is it? And what is a joke?"

"As you please, Brian. He's your son, you know." Her voice was clear, level, disapproving.

"Exactly! And you're trying to make a molly-coddle out of him. Well, just let me tell you, I won't have it. And you needn't think I'm going to let you change him to some nice kindergarten kind of a school because he's getting a little necessary education. I won't! He'll stay right where he is. The sooner and the more he learns about sex, the better for him. And most certainly if he learns that it's a grand joke, the greatest in the world. It'll keep him from lots of disappointments later on."

Irene didn't answer.

They reached the printing-shop. She got out, emphatically slamming the car's door behind her. There was a piercing agony of misery in her heart. She hadn't intended to behave like this, but her extreme resentment at his attitude, the sense of having been wilfully misunderstood and reproved, drove her to fury.

Inside the shop, she stilled the trembling of her lips and drove back her rising anger. Her business transacted, she came back to the car in a chastened mood. But against the armour of Brian's stubborn silence she heard herself saying in a calm, metallic voice: "I don't believe I'll go back just now. I've remembered that I've got to do something about getting something decent to wear. I haven't a rag that's fit to be seen. I'll take the bus downtown."

Brian merely doffed his hat in that maddening polite way which so successfully curbed and yet revealed his temper.

"Good-bye," she said bitingly. "Thanks for the lift," and turned towards the avenue.

What, she wondered contritely, was she to do next? She was vexed with herself for having chosen, as it had turned out, so clumsy an opening for what she had intended to suggest: some European school for Junior next year, and Brian to take him over. If she had been able to present her plan, and he had accepted it, as she was sure that he would have done, with other more favourable opening methods, he would have had that to look forward to as a break in the easy monotony that seemed, for some reason she was wholly unable to grasp, so hateful to him.

She was even more vexed at her own explosion of anger. What could have got into her to give way to it in such a moment?

Gradually her mood passed. She drew back from the failure of her first attempt at substitution, not so much discouraged as disappointed and ashamed. It might be, she reflected, that, in addition to her ill-timed loss of temper, she had been too hasty in her eagerness to distract him, had rushed too closely on the heels of his outburst, and had thus aroused his suspicions and his obstinacy. She had but to wait. Another more appropriate time would come, tomorrow, next week, next month. It wasn't now, as it had been once, that she was afraid that he would throw everything aside and rush off to that remote place of his heart's desire. He wouldn't, she knew. He was fond of her, loved her, in his slightly undemonstrative way.

And there were the boys.

It was only that she wanted him to be happy, resenting, however, his inability to be so with things as they were, and never acknowledging that though she did want him to be happy, it was only in her own way and by some plan of hers for him that she truly desired him to be so. Nor did she admit that all other plans, all other ways, she regarded as menaces, more or less indirect, to that security of place and substance which she insisted upon for her sons and in a lesser degree for herself.

TWO

Five days had gone by since Clare Kendry's appealing letter. Irene Redfield had not replied to it. Nor had she had any other word from Clare.

She had not carried out her first intention of writing at once because on going back to the letter for Clare's address, she had come upon something which, in the rigour of her determination to maintain unbroken between them the wall that Clare herself had raised, she had forgotten, or not fully noted. It was the fact that Clare had requested her to direct her answer to the post office's general delivery.

That had angered Irene, and increased her disdain and contempt for the other.

Tearing the letter across, she had flung it into the scrap-basket. It wasn't so much Clare's carefulness and her desire for secrecy in their relations—Irene understood the need for that—as that Clare should have doubted her discretion, implied that she might not be cautious in the wording of her reply and the choice of a posting-box. Having always had complete confidence in her own good judgment and tact, Irene couldn't bear to have anyone seem to question them. Certainly not Clare Kendry.

In another, calmer moment she decided that it was, after all, better to answer nothing, to explain nothing, to refuse nothing; to dispose of the matter simply by not writing at all. Clare, of whom it couldn't be said that she was stupid, would not mistake the implication of that silence. She might—and Irene was sure that she would—choose to ignore it and write again, but that didn't matter. The whole thing would be very easy. The basket for all letters, silence for their answers.

Most likely she and Clare would never meet again. Well, she, for one, could endure that. Since childhood their lives had never really touched. Actually they were strangers. Strangers in their ways and means of living. Strangers in their desires and ambitions. Strangers even in their racial consciousness. Between them the barrier was just as high, just as broad, and just as firm as if in Clare did not run that strain of black blood. In truth, it was higher, broader, and firmer; because for her there were perils, not known, or imagined, by those others who had no such secrets to alarm or endanger them.

The day was getting on toward evening. It was past the middle of October. There had been a week of cold rain, drenching the rotting leaves which had fallen from the poor trees that lined the street on which the Redfields' house was located, and sending a damp air of penetrating chill into the house, with a hint of cold days to come. In Irene's room a low fire was burning. Outside, only a dull grey light was left of the day. Inside, lamps had already been lighted.

From the floor above there was the sound of young voices. Sometimes Junior's serious and positive; again, Ted's deceptively gracious one. Often there was laughter, or the noise of commotion, tussling, or toys being slammed down.

Junior, tall for his age, was almost incredibly like his father in feature and colouring; but his temperament was hers, practical and determined, rather than Brian's. Ted, speculative and withdrawn, was, apparently, less positive in his ideas and desires. About him there was a deceiving air of candour that was, Irene knew, like his father's show of reasonable acquiescence. If, for the time being, and with a charming appearance of artlessness, he submitted to the force of superior strength, or some other immovable condition or circumstance, it was because of his intense dislike of scenes and unpleasant argument. Brian over again.

Gradually Irene's thought slipped away from Junior and Ted, to become wholly absorbed in their father.

The old fear, with strength increased, the fear for the future, had again laid its hand on her. And, try as she might, she could not shake it off. It was as if she had admitted to herself that against that easy surface of her husband's concordance with her wishes, which had, since the war had given him back to her physically unimpaired, covered an increasing inclination to tear himself and his possessions loose from their proper setting, she was helpless.

The chagrin which she had felt at her first failure to subvert this latest manifestation of his discontent had receded, leaving in its wake an uneasy depression. Were all her efforts, all her labours, to make up to him that one loss, all her silent striving to prove to him that her way had been best, all her ministrations to him, all her outward sinking of self, to count for nothing in some unperceived sudden moment? And if so, what, then, would be the consequences to the boys? To her? To Brian himself? Endless searching had brought no answer to these questions. There was only an intense weariness from their shuttle-like procession in her brain.

The noise and commotion from above grew increasingly louder. Irene was about to go to the stairway and request the boys to be quieter in their play when she heard the doorbell ringing.

Now, who was that likely to be? She listened to Zulena's heels, faintly tapping on their way to the door, then to the shifting sound of her feet on the steps, then to her light knock on the bedroom door.

"Yes. Come in," Irene told her.

Zulena stood in the doorway. She said: "Someone to see you, Mrs. Redfield." Her tone was discreetly regretful, as if to convey that she was reluctant to disturb her mistress at that hour, and for a stranger. "A Mrs. Bellew."

Clare!

"Oh dear! Tell her, Zulena," Irene began, "that I can't— No. I'll see her. Please bring her up here."

She heard Zulena pass down the hall, down the stairs, then stood up, smoothing out the tumbled green and ivory draperies of her dress with light stroking pats. At the mirror she dusted a little powder on her nose and brushed out her hair.

She meant to tell Clare Kendry at once, and definitely, that it was of no use, her coming, that she couldn't be responsible, that she'd talked it over with Brian, who had agreed with her that it was wiser, for Clare's own sake, to refrain—

But that was as far as she got in her rehearsal. For Clare had come softly into the room without knocking, and before Irene could greet her, had dropped a kiss on her dark curls.

Looking at the woman before her, Irene Redfield had a sudden inexplicable onrush of affectionate feeling. Reaching out, she grasped Clare's two hands in her own and cried with something like awe in her voice: "Dear God! But aren't you lovely, Clare!"

Clare tossed that aside. Like the furs and small blue hat which she threw on the bed before seating herself slantwise in Irene's favourite chair, with one foot curled under her.

"Didn't you mean to answer my letter, 'Rene?" she asked gravely.

Irene looked away. She had that uncomfortable feeling that one has when one has not been wholly kind or wholly true.

Clare went on: "Every day I went to that nasty little post-office place. I'm sure they were all beginning to think that I'd been carrying on an illicit love-affair and that the man had thrown me over. Every morning the same answer: 'Nothing for you.' I got into an awful fright, thinking that something might have happened to your letter, or to mine. And half the nights I would lie awake looking out at the watery stars— hopeless things, the stars—worrying and wondering. But at last it soaked in, that you hadn't written and didn't intend to. And then—well, as soon as ever I'd seen Jack off for Florida, I came straight here. And now, 'Rene, please tell me quite frankly why you didn't answer my letter."

"Because, you see—" Irene broke off and kept Clare waiting while she lit a cigarette, blew out the match, and dropped it into a tray. She was trying to collect her arguments, for some sixth sense warned her that it was going to be harder than she thought to convince Clare Kendry of the folly of Harlem for her. Finally she proceeded: "I can't help thinking that you ought not to come up here, ought not to run the risk of knowing Negroes."

"You mean you don't want me, 'Rene?"

Irene hadn't supposed that anyone could look so hurt. She said, quite gently, "No, Clare, it's not that. But even you must see that it's terribly foolish, and not just the right thing."

The tinkle of Clare's laugh rang out, while she passed her hands over the bright sweep of her hair. "Oh, 'Rene!" she cried, "you're priceless! And you haven't changed a bit. The right thing!" Leaning forward, she looked curiously into Irene's disapproving brown eyes. "You don't, you really can't mean exactly that! Nobody could. It's simply unbelievable."

Irene was on her feet before she realized that she had risen. "What I really mean," she retorted, "is that it's dangerous and that you ought not to run such silly risks. No one ought to. You least of all."

Her voice was brittle. For into her mind had come a thought, strange and irrelevant, a suspicion, that had surprised and shocked her and driven her to her feet. It was that in spite of her determined selfishness the woman before her was yet capable of heights and depths of feeling that she, Irene Redfield, had never known. Indeed, never cared to know. The thought, the suspicion, was gone as quickly as it had come.

Clare said: "Oh, me!"

Irene touched her arm caressingly, as if in contrition for that flashing thought. "Yes, Clare, you. It's not safe. Not safe at all."

"Safe!"

It seemed to Irene that Clare had snapped her teeth down on the word and then flung it from her. And for another flying second she had that suspicion of Clare's ability for a quality of feeling that was to her strange, and even repugnant. She was aware, too, of a dim premonition of some impending disaster. It was as if Clare Kendry had said to her, for whom safety, security, were all-important: "Safe! Damn being safe!" and meant it.

With a gesture of impatience she sat down. In a voice of cool formality, she said: "Brian and I have talked the whole thing over carefully and decided that it isn't wise. He says it's always a dangerous business, this coming back. He's seen more than one come to grief because of it. And, Clare, considering everything—Mr. Bellew's attitude and all that—don't you think you ought to be as careful as you can?"

Clare's deep voice broke the small silence that had followed Irene's speech. She said, speaking almost plaintively: "I ought to have known. It's Jack. I don't blame you for being angry, though I must say you behaved beautifully that day. But I did think you'd understand, 'Rene. It was that, partly, that has made me want to see other people. It just swooped down and changed everything. If it hadn't been for that, I'd have gone on to the end, never seeing any of you. But that did something to me, and I've been so lonely since! You can't know. Not close to a single soul. Never anyone to really talk to."

Irene pressed out her cigarette. While doing so, she saw again the vision of Clare Kendry staring disdainfully down at the face of her father, and thought that it would be like that that she would look at her husband if he lay dead before her.

Her own resentment was swept aside and her voice held an accent of pity as she exclaimed: "Why, Clare! I didn't know. Forgive me. I feel like seven beasts. It was stupid of me not to realize."

"No. Not at all. You couldn't. Nobody, none of you, could," Clare moaned. The black eyes filled with tears that ran down her cheeks and spilled into her lap, ruining the priceless velvet of her dress. Her long hands were a little uplifted and clasped tightly together. Her effort to speak moderately was obvious, but not successful. "How could you know? How could you? You're free. You're happy. And," with faint derision, "safe."

Irene passed over that touch of derision, for the poignant rebellion of the other's words had brought the tears to her own eyes, though she didn't allow them to fall. The truth was that she knew weeping did not become her. Few women, she imagined, wept as attractively as Clare. "I'm beginning to believe," she murmured, "that no one is ever completely happy, or free, or safe."

"Well, then, what does it matter? One risk more or less, if

we're not safe anyway, if even you're not, it can't make all the difference in the world. It can't to me. Besides, I'm used to risks. And this isn't such a big one as you're trying to make it."

"Oh, but it is. And it can make all the difference in the world. There's your little girl, Clare. Think of the consequences to her."

Clare's face took on a startled look, as though she were totally unprepared for this new weapon with which Irene had assailed her. Seconds passed, during which she sat with stricken eyes and compressed lips. "I think," she said at last, "that being a mother is the cruellest thing in the world." Her clasped hands swayed forward and back again, and her scarlet mouth trembled irrepressibly.

"Yes," Irene softly agreed. For a moment she was unable to say more, so accurately had Clare put into words that which, not so definitely defined, was so often in her own heart of late. At the same time she was conscious that here, to her hand, was a reason which could not be lightly brushed aside. "Yes," she repeated, "and the most responsible, Clare. We mothers are all responsible for the security and happiness of our children. Think what it would mean to your Margery if Mr. Bellew should find out. You'd probably lose her. And even if you didn't, nothing that concerned her would ever be the same again. He'd never forget that she had Negro blood. And if she should learn—Well, I believe that after twelve it is too late to learn a thing like that. She'd never forgive you. You may be used to risks, but this is one you mustn't take, Clare. It's a selfish whim, an unnecessary and—"

"Yes, Zulena, what is it?" she inquired, a trifle tartly, of the servant who had silently materialized in the doorway.

"The telephone's for you, Mrs. Redfield. It's Mr. Wentworth."[1]

"All right. Thank you. I'll take it here." And, with a muttered apology to Clare, she took up the instrument.

"Hello. . . . Yes, Hugh. . . . Oh, quite. . . . And you? . . . I'm sorry, every single thing's gone. . . . Oh, too bad. . . . Ye-es, I s'pose you could. Not very pleasant, though. . . . Yes, of course, in a pinch everything goes. . . . Wait! I've got it! I'll change

mine with whoever's next to you, and you can have that. . . .
No. . . . I mean it. . . . I'll be so busy I shan't know whether
I'm sitting or standing. . . . As long as Brian has a place to
drop down now and then. . . . Not a single soul. . . . No,
don't. . . . That's nice. . . . My love to Bianca. . . . I'll see to it
right away and call you back. . . . Good-bye."

She hung up and turned back to Clare, a little frown on her
softly chiselled features. "It's the N. W. L. dance," she explained, "the Negro Welfare League,[2] you know. I'm on the
ticket committee, or, rather, I *am* the committee. Thank heaven
it comes off tomorrow night and doesn't happen again for a
year. I'm about crazy, and now I've got to persuade somebody
to change boxes with me."

"That wasn't," Clare asked, "Hugh Wentworth? Not *the*
Hugh Wentworth?"

Irene inclined her head. On her face was a tiny triumphant
smile. "Yes, *the* Hugh Wentworth. D'you know him?"

"No. How should I? But I do know about him. And I've
read a book or two of his."

"Awfully good, aren't they?"

"U-umm, I s'pose so. Sort of contemptuous, I thought. As
if he more or less despised everything and everybody."

"I shouldn't be a bit surprised if he did. Still, he's about
earned the right to. Lived on the edges of nowhere in at least
three continents. Been through every danger in all kinds of
savage places. It's no wonder he thinks the rest of us are a lazy
self-pampering lot. Hugh's a dear, though, generous as one of
the twelve disciples; give you the shirt off his back. Bianca—
that's his wife—is nice too."

"And he's coming up here to your dance?"

Irene asked why not.

"It seems rather curious, a man like that, going to a Negro
dance."

This, Irene told her, was the year 1927 in the city of New
York, and hundreds of white people of Hugh Wentworth's
type came to affairs in Harlem, more all the time. So many
that Brian had said: "Pretty soon the coloured people won't
be allowed in at all, or will have to sit in Jim Crowed sections."

"What do they come for?"

"Same reason you're here, to see Negroes."

"But why?"

"Various motives," Irene explained. "A few purely and frankly to enjoy themselves. Others to get material to turn into shekels.[3] More, to gaze on these great and near great while they gaze on the Negroes."

Clare clapped her hands. "'Rene, suppose I come too! It sounds terribly interesting and amusing. And I don't see why I shouldn't."

Irene, who was regarding her through narrowed eyelids, had the same thought that she had had two years ago on the roof of the Drayton, that Clare Kendry was just a shade too good-looking. Her tone was on the edge of irony as she said: "You mean because so many other white people go?"

A pale rose-colour came into Clare's ivory cheeks. She lifted a hand in protest. "Don't be silly! Certainly not! I mean that in a crowd of that kind I shouldn't be noticed."

On the contrary, was Irene's opinion. It might be even doubly dangerous. Some friend or acquaintance of John Bellew or herself might see and recognize her.

At that, Clare laughed for a long time, little musical trills following one another in sequence after sequence. It was as if the thought of any friend of John Bellew's going to a Negro dance was to her the most amusing thing in the world.

"I don't think," she said, when she had done laughing, "we need worry about that."

Irene, however, wasn't so sure. But all her efforts to dissuade Clare were useless. To her, "You never can tell whom you're likely to meet there," Clare's rejoinder was: "I'll take my chance on getting by."

"Besides, you won't know a soul and I shall be too busy to look after you. You'll be bored stiff."

"I won't, I won't. If nobody asks me to dance, not even Dr. Redfield, I'll just sit and gaze on the great and the near great, too. Do, 'Rene, be polite and invite me."

Irene turned away from the caress of Clare's smile, saying promptly and positively: "I will not."

"I mean to go anyway," Clare retorted, and her voice was no less positive than Irene's.

"Oh, no. You couldn't possibly go there alone. It's a public thing. All sorts of people go, anybody who can pay a dollar, even ladies of easy virtue looking for trade. If you were to go there alone, you might be mistaken for one of them, and that wouldn't be too pleasant."

Clare laughed again. "Thanks. I never have been. It might be amusing. I'm warning you, 'Rene, that if you're not going to be nice and take me, I'll still be among those present. I suppose, my dollar's as good as anyone's."

"Oh, the dollar! Don't be a fool, Clare. I don't care where you go, or what you do. All I'm concerned with is the unpleasantness and possible danger which your going might incur, because of your situation. To put it frankly, I shouldn't like to be mixed up in any row of the kind." She had risen again as she spoke and was standing at the window lifting and spreading the small yellow chrysanthemums in the grey stone jar on the sill. Her hands shook slightly, for she was in a near rage of impatience and exasperation.

Clare's face looked strange, as if she wanted to cry again. One of her satin-covered feet swung restlessly back and forth. She said vehemently, violently almost: "Damn Jack! He keeps me out of everything. Everything I want. I could kill him! I expect I shall, some day."

"I wouldn't," Irene advised her, "you see, there's still capital punishment, in this state at least. And really, Clare, after everything's said, I can't see that you've a right to put all the blame on him. You've got to admit that there's his side to the thing. You didn't tell him you were coloured, so he's got no way of knowing about this hankering of yours after Negroes, or that it galls you to fury to hear them called niggers and black devils. As far as I can see, you'll just have to endure some things and give up others. As we've said before, everything must be paid for. Do, please, be reasonable."

But Clare, it was plain, had shut away reason as well as caution. She shook her head. "I can't, I can't," she said. "I would if I could, but I can't. You don't know, you can't realize how

I want to see Negroes, to be with them again, to talk with them, to hear them laugh."

And in the look she gave Irene, there was something groping, and hopeless, and yet so absolutely determined that it was like an image of the futile searching and the firm resolution in Irene's own soul, and increased the feeling of doubt and compunction that had been growing within her about Clare Kendry.

She gave in.

"Oh, come if you want to. I s'pose you're right. Once can't do such a terrible lot of harm."

Pushing aside Clare's extravagant thanks, for immediately she was sorry that she had consented, she said briskly: "Should you like to come up and see my boys?"

"I'd love to."

They went up, Irene thinking that Brian would consider that she'd behaved like a spineless fool. And he would be right. She certainly had.

Clare was smiling. She stood in the doorway of the boys' playroom, her shadowy eyes looking down on Junior and Ted, who had sprung apart from their tusselling. Junior's face had a funny little look of resentment. Ted's was blank.

Clare said: "Please don't be cross. Of course, I know I've gone and spoiled everything. But maybe, if I promise not to get too much in the way, you'll let me come in, just the same."

"Sure, come in if you want to," Ted told her. "We can't stop you, you know." He smiled and made her a little bow and then turned away to a shelf that held his favourite books. Taking one down, he settled himself in a chair and began to read.

Junior said nothing, did nothing, merely stood there waiting.

"Get up, Ted! That's rude. This is Theodore, Mrs. Bellew. Please excuse his bad manners. He does know better. And this is Brian junior. Mrs. Bellew is an old friend of mother's. We used to play together when we were little girls."

Clare had gone and Brian had telephoned that he'd been detained and would have his dinner downtown. Irene was a little glad for that. She was going out later herself, and that meant she wouldn't, probably, see Brian until morning and so could put off for a few more hours speaking of Clare and the N. W. L. dance.

She was angry with herself and with Clare. But more with herself, for having permitted Clare to tease her into doing something that Brian had, all but expressly, asked her not to do. She didn't want him ruffled, not just then, not while he was possessed of that unreasonable restless feeling.

She was annoyed, too, because she was aware that she had consented to something which, if it went beyond the dance, would involve her in numerous petty inconveniences and eva-sions. And not only at home with Brian, but outside with friends and acquaintances. The disagreeable possibilities in connection with Clare Kendry's coming among them loomed before her in endless irritating array.

Clare, it seemed, still retained her ability to secure the thing that she wanted in the face of any opposition, and in utter disregard of the convenience and desire of others. About her there was some quality, hard and persistent, with the strength and endurance of rock, that would not be beaten or ignored. She couldn't, Irene thought, have had an entirely serene life. Not with that dark secret for ever crouching in the background of her consciousness. And yet she hadn't the air of a woman whose life had been touched by uncertainty or suffering. Pain, fear, and grief were things that left their mark on people. Even love, that exquisite torturing emotion, left its subtle traces on the countenance.

But Clare—she had remained almost what she had always been, an attractive, somewhat lonely child—selfish, wilful, and disturbing.

THREE

The things which Irene Redfield remembered afterward about the Negro Welfare League dance seemed, to her, unimportant and unrelated.

She remembered the not quite derisive smile with which Brian had cloaked his vexation when she informed him—oh, so apologetically—that she had promised to take Clare, and related the conversation of her visit.

She remembered her own little choked exclamation of admiration, when, on coming downstairs a few minutes later than she had intended, she had rushed into the living-room where Brian was waiting and had found Clare there too. Clare, exquisite, golden, fragrant, flaunting, in a stately gown of shining black taffeta, whose long, full skirt lay in graceful folds about her slim golden feet; her glistening hair drawn smoothly back into a small twist at the nape of her neck; her eyes sparkling like dark jewels. Irene, with her new rose-coloured chiffon frock ending at the knees, and her cropped curls, felt dowdy and commonplace. She regretted that she hadn't counselled Clare to wear something ordinary and inconspicuous. What on earth would Brian think of deliberate courting of attention? But if Clare Kendry's appearance had in it anything that was, to Brian Redfield, annoying or displeasing, the fact was not discernible to his wife as, with an uneasy feeling of guilt, she stood there looking into his face while Clare explained that she and he had made their own introductions, accompanying her words with a little deferential smile for Brian, and receiving in return one of his amused, slightly mocking smiles.

She remembered Clare's saying, as they sped northward: "You know, I feel exactly as I used to on the Sunday we went to the Christmas-tree celebration. I knew there was to be a surprise for me and couldn't quite guess what it was to be. I am *so* excited. You can't possibly imagine! It's marvellous to be really on the way! I can hardly believe it!"

At her words and tone a chilly wave of scorn had crept through Irene. All those superlatives! She said, taking care to speak indifferently: "Well, maybe in some ways you will be surprised, more, probably, than you anticipate."

Brian, at the wheel, had thrown back: "And then again, she won't be so very surprised after all, for it'll no doubt be about what she expects. Like the Christmas-tree."

She remembered rushing around here and there, consulting with this person and that one, and now and then snatching a part of a dance with some man whose dancing she particularly liked.

She remembered catching glimpses of Clare in the whirling crowd, dancing, sometimes with a white man, more often with a Negro, frequently with Brian. Irene was glad that he was being nice to Clare, and glad that Clare was having the opportunity to discover that some coloured men were superior to some white men.

She remembered a conversation she had with Hugh Wentworth in a free half-hour when she had dropped into a chair in an emptied box and let her gaze wander over the bright crowd below.

Young men, old men, white men, black men; youthful women, older women, pink women, golden women; fat men, thin men, tall men, short men; stout women, slim women, stately women, small women moved by. An old nursery rhyme popped into her head. She turned to Wentworth, who had just taken a seat beside her, and recited it:

> "*Rich man, poor man,*
> *Beggar man, thief,*
> *Doctor, lawyer,*
> *Indian chief.*"

"Yes," Wentworth said, "that's it. Everybody seems to be here and a few more. But what I'm trying to find out is the name, status, and race of the blonde beauty out of the fairy-tale. She's dancing with Ralph Hazelton at the moment. Nice study in contrasts, that."

It was. Clare fair and golden, like a sunlit day. Hazelton dark, with gleaming eyes, like a moonlit night.

"She's a girl I used to know a long time ago in Chicago. And she wanted especially to meet you."

"'S awfully good of her, I'm sure. And now, alas! the usual thing's happened. All these others, these—er—'gentlemen of colour' have driven a mere Nordic from her mind."

"Stuff!"

"'S a fact, and what happens to all the ladies of my superior race who're lured up here. Look at Bianca. Have I laid eyes on her tonight except in spots, here and there, being twirled about by some Ethiopian? I have not."

"But, Hugh, you've got to admit that the average coloured man is a better dancer than the average white man—that is, if the celebrities and 'butter and egg' men[1] who find their way up here are fair specimens of white Terpsichorean art."

"Not having tripped the light fantastic[2] with any of the males, I'm not in a position to argue the point. But I don't think it's merely that. 'S something else, some other attraction. They're always raving about the good looks of some Negro, preferably an unusually dark one. Take Hazelton there, for example. Dozens of women have declared him to be fascinatingly handsome. How about you, Irene? Do you think he's—er—ravishingly beautiful?"

"I do not! And I don't think the others do either. Not honestly, I mean. I think that what they feel is—well, a kind of emotional excitement. You know, the sort of thing you feel in the presence of something strange, and even, perhaps, a bit repugnant to you; something so different that it's really at the opposite end of the pole from all your accustomed notions of beauty."

"Damned if I don't think you're halfway right!"

"I'm sure I am. Completely. (Except, of course, when it's just patronizing kindness on their part.) And I know coloured girls who've experienced the same thing—the other way round, naturally."

"And the men? You don't subscribe to the general opinion about their reason for coming up here. Purely predatory. Or, do you?"

"N-no. More curious, I should say."

Wentworth, whose eyes were a clouded amber colour, had given her a long, searching look that was really a stare. He said: "All this is awfully interestin', Irene. We've got to have a long talk about it some time soon. There's your friend from Chicago, first time up here and all that. A case in point."

Irene's smile had only just lifted the corners of her painted lips. A match blazed in Wentworth's broad hands as he lighted her cigarette and his own, and flickered out before he asked: "Or isn't she?"

Her smile changed to a laugh. "Oh, Hugh! You're so clever. You usually know everything. Even how to tell the sheep from the goats. What do you think? Is she?"

He blew a long contemplative wreath of smoke. "Damned if I know! I'll be as sure as anything that I've learned the trick. And then in the next minute I'll find I couldn't pick some of 'em if my life depended on it."

"Well, don't let that worry you. Nobody can. Not by look-ing."

"Not by looking, eh? Meaning?"

"I'm afraid I can't explain. Not clearly. There are ways. But they're not definite or tangible."

"Feeling of kinship, or something like that?"

"Good heavens, no! Nobody has that, except for their in-laws."

"Right again! But go on about the sheep and the goats."

"Well, take my own experience with Dorothy Thompkins.[3] I'd met her four or five times, in groups and crowds of people, before I knew she wasn't a Negro. One day I went to an awful tea, terribly dicty.[4] Dorothy was there. We got talking. In less than five minutes, I knew she was 'fay.'[5] Not from anything she did or said or anything in her appearance. Just—just some-thing. A thing that couldn't be registered."

"Yes, I understand what you mean. Yet lots of people 'pass' all the time."

"Not on our side, Hugh. It's easy for a Negro to 'pass' for white. But I don't think it would be so simple for a white person to 'pass' for coloured."

"Never thought of that."

"No, you wouldn't. Why should you?"

He regarded her critically through mists of smoke. "Slippin' me, Irene?"[6]

She said soberly: "Not you, Hugh. I'm too fond of you. And you're too sincere."

And she remembered that towards the end of the dance Brian had come to her and said: "I'll drop you first and then run Clare down." And that he had been doubtful of her discretion when she had explained to him that he wouldn't have to bother because she had asked Bianca Wentworth to take her down with them. Did she, he had asked, think it had been wise to tell them about Clare?

"I told them nothing," she said sharply, for she was unbearably tired, "except that she was at the Walsingham. It's on their way. And, really, I haven't thought anything about the wisdom of it, but now that I do, I'd say it's much better for them to take her than you."

"As you please. She's your friend, you know," he had answered, with a disclaiming shrug of his shoulders.

Except for these few unconnected things the dance faded to a blurred memory, its outlines mingling with those of other dances of its kind that she had attended in the past and would attend in the future.

FOUR

But undistinctive as the dance had seemed, it was, nevertheless, important. For it marked the beginning of a new factor
in Irene Redfield's life, something that left its trace on all the
future years of her existence. It was the beginning of a new
friendship with Clare Kendry.

She came to them frequently after that. Always with a touch-
ing gladness that welled up and overflowed on all the Redfield
household. Yet Irene could never be sure whether her comings
were a joy or a vexation.

Certainly she was no trouble. She had not to be entertained,
or even noticed—if anyone could ever avoid noticing Clare. If
Irene happened to be out or occupied, Clare could very happily amuse herself with Ted and Junior, who had conceived
for her an admiration that verged on adoration, especially Ted.
Or, lacking the boys, she would descend to the kitchen and,
with—to Irene—an exasperating childlike lack of perception,
spend her visit in talk and merriment with Zulena and Sadie.

Irene, while secretly resenting these visits to the playroom
and kitchen, for some obscure reason which she shied away
from putting into words, never requested that Clare make an
end of them, or hinted that she wouldn't have spoiled her own
Margery so outrageously, nor been so friendly with white
servants.

Brian looked on these things with the same tolerant amusement that marked his entire attitude toward Clare. Never since
his faintly derisive surprise at Irene's information that she was
to go with them the night of the dance, had he shown any dis-
approval of Clare's presence. On the other hand, it couldn't

be said that her presence seemed to please him. It didn't annoy or disturb him, so far as Irene could judge. That was all.

Didn't he, she once asked him, think Clare was extraordinarily beautiful?

"No," he had answered. "That is, not particularly."

"Brian, you're fooling!"

"No, honestly. Maybe I'm fussy. I s'pose she'd be an unusually good-looking white woman. I like my ladies darker. Beside an A-number-one sheba, she simply hasn't got 'em."

Clare went, sometimes with Irene and Brian, to parties and dances, and on a few occasions when Irene hadn't been able or inclined to go out, she had gone alone with Brian to some bridge party or benefit dance.

Once in a while she came formally to dine with them. She wasn't, however, in spite of her poise and air of worldliness, the ideal dinner-party guest. Beyond the æsthetic pleasure one got from watching her, she contributed little, sitting for the most part silent, an odd dreaming look in her hypnotic eyes. Though she could for some purpose of her own—the desire to be included in some party being made up to go cabareting, or an invitation to a dance or a tea—talk fluently and entertainingly.

She was generally liked. She was so friendly and responsive, and so ready to press the sweet food of flattery on all. Nor did she object to appearing a bit pathetic and ill-used, so that people could feel sorry for her. And, no matter how often she came among them, she still remained someone apart, a little mysterious and strange, someone to wonder about and to admire and to pity.

Her visits were undecided and uncertain, being, as they were, dependent on the presence or absence of John Bellew in the city. But she did, once in a while, manage to steal uptown for an afternoon even when he was not away. As time went on without any apparent danger of discovery, even Irene ceased to be perturbed about the possibility of Clare's husband's stumbling on her racial identity.

The daughter, Margery, had been left in Switzerland in

school, for Clare and Bellew would be going back in the early spring. In March, Clare thought. "And how I do hate to think of it!" she would say, always with a suggestion of leashed rebellion; "but I can't see how I'm going to get out of it. Jack won't hear of my staying behind. If I could have just a couple of months more in New York, alone I mean, I'd be the happiest thing in the world."

"I imagine you'll be happy enough, once you get away," Irene told her one day when she was bewailing her approaching departure. "Remember, there's Margery. Think how glad you'll be to see her after all this time."

"Children aren't everything," was Clare Kendry's answer to that. "There are other things in the world, though I admit some people don't seem to suspect it." And she laughed, more, it seemed, at some secret joke of her own than at her words.

Irene replied: "You know you don't mean that, Clare. You're only trying to tease me. I know very well that I take being a mother rather seriously. I *am* wrapped up in my boys and the running of my house. I can't help it. And, really, I don't think it's anything to laugh at." And though she was aware of the slight primness in her words and attitude, she had neither power nor wish to efface it.

Clare, suddenly very sober and sweet, said: "You're right. It's no laughing matter. It's shameful of me to tease you, 'Rene. You are so good." And she reached out and gave Irene's hand an affectionate little squeeze. "Don't think," she added, "whatever happens, that I'll ever forget how good you've been to me."

"Nonsense!"

"Oh, but you have, you have. It's just that I haven't any proper morals or sense of duty, as you have, that makes me act as I do."

"Now you are talking nonsense."

"But it's true, 'Rene. Can't you realize that I'm not like you a bit? Why, to get the things I want badly enough, I'd do anything, hurt anybody, throw anything away. Really, 'Rene, I'm not safe." Her voice as well as the look on her face had a beseeching earnestness that made Irene vaguely uncomfortable.

She said: "I don't believe it. In the first place what you're saying is so utterly, so wickedly wrong. And as for your giving up things—" She stopped, at a loss for an acceptable term to express her opinion of Clare's "having" nature.

But Clare Kendry had begun to cry, audibly, with no effort at restraint, and for no reason that Irene could discover.

PART THREE

FINALE

ONE

The year was getting on towards its end. October, November had gone. December had come and brought with it a little snow and then a freeze and after that a thaw and some soft pleasant days that had in them a feeling of spring.

It wasn't, this mild weather, a bit Christmasy, Irene Redfield was thinking, as she turned out of Seventh Avenue into her own street. She didn't like it to be warm and springy when it should have been cold and crisp, or grey and cloudy as if snow was about to fall. The weather, like people, ought to enter into the spirit of the season. Here the holidays were almost upon them, and the streets through which she had come were streaked with rills of muddy water and the sun shone so warmly that children had taken off their hats and scarfs. It was all as soft, as like April, as possible. The kind of weather for Easter. Certainly not for Christmas.

Though, she admitted, reluctantly, she herself didn't feel the proper Christmas spirit this year, either. But that couldn't be helped, it seemed, any more than the weather. She was weary and depressed. And for all her trying, she couldn't be free of that dull, indefinite misery which with increasing tenaciousness had laid hold of her. The morning's aimless wandering through the teeming Harlem streets, long after she had ordered the flowers which had been her excuse for setting out, was but another effort to tear herself loose from it.

She went up the cream stone steps, into the house, and down to the kitchen. There were to be people in to tea. But that, she found, after a few words with Sadie and Zulena, need give her no concern. She was thankful. She didn't want to be bothered. She went upstairs and took off her things and got into bed.

She thought: "Bother those people coming to tea!"

She thought: "If I could only be sure that at bottom it's just Brazil."

She thought: "Whatever it is, if I only knew what it was, I could manage it."

Brian again. Unhappy, restless, withdrawn. And she, who had prided herself on knowing his moods, their causes and their remedies, had found it first unthinkable, and then intolerable, that this, so like and yet so unlike those other spasmodic restlessnesses of his, should be to her incomprehensible and elusive.

He was restless and he was not restless. He was discontented, yet there were times when she felt he was possessed of some intense secret satisfaction, like a cat who had stolen the cream. He was irritable with the boys, especially Junior, for Ted, who seemed to have an uncanny knowledge of his father's periods of off moods, kept out of his way when possible. They got on his nerves, drove him to violent outbursts of temper, very different from his usual gently sarcastic remarks that constituted his idea of discipline for them. On the other hand, with her he was more than customarily considerate and abstemious. And it had been weeks since she had felt the keen edge of his irony.

He was like a man marking time, waiting. But what was he waiting for? It was extraordinary that, after all these years of accurate perception, she now lacked the talent to discover what that appearance of waiting meant. It was the knowledge that, for all her watching, all her patient study, the reason for his humour still eluded her which filled her with foreboding dread. That guarded reserve of his seemed to her unjust, inconsiderate, and alarming. It was as if he had stepped out beyond her reach into some section, strange and walled, where she could not get at him.

She closed her eyes, thinking what a blessing it would be if she could get a little sleep before the boys came in from school. She couldn't, of course, though she was so tired, having had, of late, so many sleepless nights. Nights filled with question-ings and premonitions.

But she did sleep—several hours.

She wakened to find Brian standing at her bedside looking down at her, an unfathomable expression in his eyes.

She said: "I must have dropped off to sleep," and watched a slender ghost of his old amused smile pass over his face.

"It's getting on to four," he told her, meaning, she knew, that she was going to be late again.

She fought back the quick answer that rose to her lips and said instead: "I'm getting right up. It was good of you to think to call me." She sat up.

He bowed. "Always the attentive husband, you see."

"Yes indeed. Thank goodness, everything's ready."

"Except you. Oh, and Clare's downstairs."

"Clare! What a nuisance! I didn't ask her. Purposely."

"I see. Might a mere man ask why? Or is the reason so sub-tly feminine that it wouldn't be understood by him?"

A little of his smile had come back. Irene, who was begin-ning to shake off some of her depression under his familiar banter, said, almost gaily: "Not at all. It just happens that this party happens to be for Hugh, and that Hugh happens not to care a great deal for Clare; therefore I, who happen to be giv-ing the party, didn't happen to ask her. Nothing could be sim-pler. Could it?"

"Nothing. It's so simple that I can easily see beyond your simple explanation and surmise that Clare, probably, just never happened to pay Hugh the admiring attention that he happens to consider no more than his just due. Simplest thing in the world."

Irene exclaimed in amazement: "Why, I thought you liked Hugh! You don't, you can't, believe anything so idiotic!"

"Well, Hugh does think he's God, you know."

"That," Irene declared, getting out of bed, "is absolutely not true. He thinks ever so much better of himself than that, as you, who know and have read him, ought to be able to guess. If you remember what a low opinion he has of God, you won't make such a silly mistake."

She went into the closet for her things and, coming back, hung her frock over the back of a chair and placed her shoes on the floor beside it. Then she sat down before her dressing-table.

Brian didn't speak. He continued to stand beside the bed, seeming to look at nothing in particular. Certainly not at her. True, his gaze was on her, but in it there was some quality that made her feel that at that moment she was no more to him than a pane of glass through which he stared. At what? She didn't know, couldn't guess. And this made her uncomfortable. Piqued her.

She said: "It just happens that Hugh prefers intelligent women."

Plainly he was startled. "D'you mean that you think Clare is stupid?" he asked, regarding her with lifted eyebrows, which emphasized the disbelief of his voice.

She wiped the cold cream from her face, before she said: "No, I don't. She isn't stupid. She's intelligent enough in a purely feminine way. Eighteenth-century France would have been a marvellous setting for her, or the old South[1] if she hadn't made the mistake of being born a Negro."

"I see. Intelligent enough to wear a tight bodice and keep bowing swains whispering compliments and retrieving dropped fans. Rather a pretty picture. I take it, though, as slightly feline in its implication."

"Well, then, all I can say is that you take it wrongly. Nobody admires Clare more than I do, for the kind of intelligence she has, as well as for her decorative qualities. But she's not— She isn't— She hasn't— Oh, I can't explain it. Take Bianca, for example, or, to keep to the race, Felise Freeland. Looks *and* brains. Real brains that can hold their own with anybody. Clare has got brains of a sort, the kind that are useful too. Acquisitive, you know. But she'd bore a man like Hugh to suicide. Still, I never thought that even Clare would come to a private party to which she hadn't been asked. But, it's like her."

For a minute there was silence. She completed the bright red arch of her full lips. Brian moved towards the door. His hand was on the knob. He said: "I'm sorry, Irene. It's my fault entirely. She seemed so hurt at being left out that I told her I was sure you'd forgotten and to just come along."

Irene cried out: "But, Brian, I—" and stopped, amazed at the fierce anger that had blazed up in her.

Brian's head came round with a jerk. His brows lifted in an odd surprise.

Her voice, she realized, *had* gone queer. But she had an instinctive feeling that it hadn't been the whole cause of his attitude. And that little straightening motion of the shoulders. Hadn't it been like that of a man drawing himself up to receive a blow? Her fright was like a scarlet spear of terror leaping at her heart.

Clare Kendry! So that was it! Impossible. It couldn't be.

In the mirror before her she saw that he was still regarding her with that air of slight amazement. She dropped her eyes to the jars and bottles on the table and began to fumble among them with hands whose fingers shook slightly.

"Of course," she said carefully, "I'm glad you did. And in spite of my recent remarks, Clare does add to any party. She's so easy on the eyes."

When she looked again, the surprise had gone from his face and the expectancy from his bearing.

"Yes," he agreed. "Well, I guess I'll run along. One of us ought to be down, I s'pose."

"You're right. One of us ought to." She was surprised that it was in her normal tones she spoke, caught as she was by the heart since that dull indefinite fear had grown suddenly into sharp panic. "I'll be down before you know it," she promised.

"All right." But he still lingered. "You're quite certain. You don't mind my asking her? Not awfully, I mean? I see now that I ought to have spoken to you. Trust women to have their reasons for everything."

She made a little pretence at looking at him, managed a tiny smile, and turned away. Clare! How sickening!

"Yes, don't they?" she said, striving to keep her voice casual. Within her she felt a hardness from feeling, not absent, but repressed. And that hardness was rising, swelling. Why didn't he go? Why didn't he?

He had opened the door at last. "You won't be long?" he asked, admonished.

She shook her head, unable to speak, for there was a choking in her throat, and the confusion in her mind was like the beating of wings. Behind her she heard the gentle impact of the door as it closed behind him, and knew that he had gone. Down to Clare.

For a long minute she sat in strained stiffness. The face in the mirror vanished from her sight, blotted out by this thing which had so suddenly flashed across her groping mind. Impossible for her to put it immediately into words or give it outline, for, prompted by some impulse of self-protection, she recoiled from exact expression.

She closed her unseeing eyes and clenched her fists. She tried not to cry. But her lips tightened and no effort could check the hot tears of rage and shame that sprang into her eyes and flowed down her cheeks; so she laid her face in her arms and wept silently.

When she was sure that she had done crying, she wiped away the warm remaining tears and got up. After bathing her swollen face in cold, refreshing water and carefully applying a stinging splash of toilet water, she went back to the mirror and regarded herself gravely. Satisfied that there lingered no betraying evidence of weeping, she dusted a little powder on her dark-white face and again examined it carefully, and with a kind of ridiculing contempt.

"I do think," she confided to it, "that you've been something— oh, very much—of a damned fool."

Downstairs the ritual of tea gave her some busy moments, and that, she decided, was a blessing. She wanted no empty spaces of time in which her mind would immediately return to that horror which she had not yet gathered sufficient courage to face. Pouring tea properly and nicely was an occupation that required a kind of well-balanced attention.

In the room beyond, a clock chimed. A single sound. Fifteen minutes past five o'clock. That was all! And yet in the short space of half an hour all of life had changed, lost its colour, its vividness, its whole meaning. No, she reflected, it wasn't that that had happened. Life about her, apparently, went on exactly as before.

"Oh, Mrs. Runyon. . . . So nice to see you. . . . Two? . . . Really? . . . How exciting! . . . Yes, I think Tuesday's all right. . . ."

Yes, life went on precisely as before. It was only she that had changed. Knowing, stumbling on this thing, had changed her. It was as if in a house long dim, a match had been struck, showing ghastly shapes where had been only blurred shadows.

Chatter, chatter, chatter. Someone asked her a question. She glanced up with what she felt was a rigid smile.

"Yes . . . Brian picked it up last winter in Haiti.[2] Terribly weird, isn't it? . . . It *is* rather marvellous in its own hideous way. . . . Practically nothing, I believe. A few cents. . . ."

Hideous. A great weariness came over her. Even the small exertion of pouring golden tea into thin old cups seemed almost too much for her. She went on pouring. Made repetitions of her smile. Answered questions. Manufactured conversation. She thought: "I feel like the oldest person in the world with the longest stretch of life before me."

"Josephine Baker? . . .[3] No. I've never seen her. . . . Well, she might have been in *Shuffle Along*[4] when I saw it, but if she was, I don't remember her. . . . Oh, but you're wrong! . . . I do think Ethel Waters[5] is awfully good. . . ."

There were the familiar little tinkling sounds of spoons striking against frail cups, the soft running sounds of inconsequential talk, punctuated now and then with laughter. In irregular small groups, disintegrating, coalescing, striking just the right note of disharmony, disorder in the big room, which Irene had furnished with a sparingness that was almost chaste, moved the guests with that slight familiarity that makes a party a success. On the floor and the walls the sinking sun threw long, fantastic shadows.

So like many other tea-parties she had had. So unlike any of those others. But she mustn't think yet. Time enough for that after. All the time in the world. She had a second's flashing knowledge of what those words might portend. Time with Brian. Time without him. It was gone, leaving in its place an almost uncontrollable impulse to laugh, to scream, to hurl things about. She wanted, suddenly, to shock people, to hurt them, to make them notice her, to be aware of her suffering.

"Hello, Dave. . . . Felise. . . . Really your clothes are the despair of half the women in Harlem. . . . How do you do it? . . . Lovely, is it Worth or Lanvin? . . . Oh, a mere Babani. . . ."

"Merely that," Felise Freeland acknowledged. "Come out of it, Irene, whatever it is. You look like the second grave-digger."

"Thanks, for the hint, Felise. I'm not feeling quite up to par. The weather, I guess."

"Buy yourself an expensive new frock, child. It always helps. Any time this child gets the blues, it means money out of Dave's pocket. How're those boys of yours?"

The boys! For once she'd forgotten them.

They were, she told Felise, very well. Felise mumbled something about that being awfully nice, and said she'd have to fly, because for a wonder she saw Mrs. Bellew sitting by herself, "and I've been trying to get her alone all afternoon. I want her for a party. Isn't she stunning today?"

Clare was. Irene couldn't remember ever having seen her look better. She was wearing a superlatively simple cinnamon-brown frock which brought out all her vivid beauty, and a little golden bowl of a hat. Around her neck hung a string of amber beads that would easily have made six or eight like one Irene owned. Yes, she was stunning.

The ripple of talk flowed on. The fire roared. The shadows stretched longer.

Across the room was Hugh. He wasn't, Irene hoped, being too bored. He seemed as he always did, a bit aloof, a little amused, and somewhat weary. And as usual he was hovering before the book-shelves. But he was not, she noticed, looking at the book he had taken down. Instead, his dull amber eyes were held by something across the room. They were a little scornful. Well, Hugh had never cared for Clare Kendry. For a minute Irene hesitated, then turned her head, though she knew what it was that held Hugh's gaze. Clare, who had suddenly clouded all her days. Brian, the father of Ted and Junior.

Clare's ivory face was what it always was, beautiful and caressing. Or maybe today a little masked. Unrevealing. Unaltered and undisturbed by any emotion within or without. Brian's seemed to Irene to be pitiably bare. Or was it too as it always was? That half-effaced seeking look, did he always have that? Queer, that now she didn't know, couldn't recall. Then she saw him smile, and the smile made his face all eager and shining. Impelled by some inner urge of loyalty to herself, she glanced away. But only for a moment. And when she turned towards them again, she thought that the look on his face was the most melancholy and yet the most scoffing that she had ever seen upon it.

In the next quarter of an hour she promised herself to Bianca Wentworth in Sixty-second Street, Jane Tenant at Seventh Avenue and a Hundred and Fiftieth Street, and the Dashields in Brooklyn for dinner all on the same evening and at almost the same hour.

Oh well, what did it matter? She had no thoughts at all now, and all she felt was a great fatigue. Before her tired eyes Clare Kendry was talking to Dave Freeland.[6] Scraps of their conversation, in Clare's husky voice, floated over to her: ". . . always admired you . . . so much about you long ago . . . everybody says so . . . no one but you. . . ." And more of the same. The man hung rapt on her words, though he was the husband of Felise Freeland, and the author of novels that revealed a man of perception and a devastating irony. And he fell for such pishposh! And all because Clare had a trick of sliding down ivory lids over astonishing black eyes and then lifting them suddenly and turning on a caressing smile. Men like Dave Freeland fell for it. And Brian.

Her mental and physical languor receded. Brian. What did it mean? How would it affect her and the boys? The boys! She had a surge of relief. It ebbed, vanished. A feeling of absolute unimportance followed. Actually, she didn't count. She was, to him, only the mother of his sons. That was all. Alone she was nothing. Worse. An obstacle.

Rage boiled up in her.

There was a slight crash. On the floor at her feet lay the

shattered cup. Dark stains dotted the bright rug. Spread. The
chatter stopped. Went on. Before her, Zulena gathered up the
white fragments.

As from a distance Hugh Wentworth's clipt voice came to
her, though he was, she was aware, somehow miraculously at
her side. "Sorry," he apologized. "Must have pushed you.
Clumsy of me. Don't tell me it's priceless and irreplaceable."

It hurt. Dear God! How the thing hurt! But she couldn't
think of that now. Not with Hugh sitting there mumbling
apologies and lies. The significance of his words, the power
of his discernment, stirred in her a sense of caution. Her pride
revolted. Damn Hugh! Something would have to be done about
him. Now. She couldn't, it seemed, help his knowing. It was
too late for that. But she could and would keep him from
knowing that she knew. She could, she would bear it. She'd
have to. There were the boys. Her whole body went taut. In
that second she saw that she could bear anything, but only if
no one knew that she had anything to bear. It hurt. It frightened her, but she could bear it.

She turned to Hugh. Shook her head. Raised innocent dark
eyes to his concerned pale ones. "Oh, no," she protested, "you
didn't push me. Cross your heart, hope to die, and I'll tell you
how it happened."

"Done!"

"Did you notice that cup? Well, you're lucky. It was the ug-
liest thing that your ancestors, the charming Confederates ever
owned. I've forgotten how many thousands of years ago it was
that Brian's great-great-grand-uncle owned it. But it has, or
had, a good old hoary history. It was brought North by way
of the subway. Oh, all right! Be English if you want to and call
it the underground. What I'm coming to is the fact that I've
never figured out a way of getting rid of it until about five
minutes ago. I had an inspiration. I had only to break it, and
I was rid of it for ever. So simple! And I'd never thought of it
before."

Hugh nodded and his frosty smile spread over his features.
Had she convinced him?

"Still," she went on with a little laugh that didn't, she was

sure, sound the least bit forced, "I'm perfectly willing for you
to take the blame and admit that you pushed me at the wrong
moment. What are friends for, if not to help bear our sins?
Brian will certainly be told that it was your fault.

"More tea, Clare? . . . I haven't had a minute with you. . . .
Yes, it is a nice party. . . . You'll stay to dinner, I hope. . . . Oh,
too bad! . . . I'll be alone with the boys. . . . They'll be sorry.
Brian's got a medical meeting, or something. . . . Nice frock
you're wearing. . . . Thanks. . . . Well, good-bye; see you soon,
I hope."

The clock chimed. One. Two. Three. Four. Five. Six. Was
it, could it be, only a little over an hour since she had come
down to tea? One little hour.

"Must you go? . . . Good-bye. . . . Thank you so much. . . .
So nice to see you. . . . Yes, Wednesday. . . . My love to
Madge. . . . Sorry, but I'm filled up for Tuesday. . . . Oh,
really? . . . Yes. . . . Good-bye. . . . Good-bye. . . ."

It hurt. It hurt like hell. But it didn't matter, if no one knew.
If everything could go on as before. If the boys were safe.

It did hurt.

But it didn't matter.

TWO

But it did matter. It mattered more than anything had ever mattered before.

What bitterness! That the one fear, the one uncertainty, that she had felt, Brian's ache to go somewhere else, should have dwindled to a childish triviality! And with it the quality of the courage and resolution with which she had met it. From the visions and dangers which she now perceived she shrank away. For them she had no remedy or courage. Desperately she tried to shut out the knowledge from which had risen this turmoil, which she had no power to moderate or still, within her. And half succeeded.

For, she reasoned, what was there, what had there been, to show that she was even half correct in her tormenting notion? Nothing. She had seen nothing, heard nothing. She had no facts or proofs. She was only making herself unutterably wretched by an unfounded suspicion. It had been a case of looking for trouble and finding it in good measure. Merely that.

With this self-assurance that she had no real knowledge, she redoubled her efforts to drive out of her mind the distressing thought of faiths broken and trusts betrayed which every mental vision of Clare, of Brian, brought with them. She could not, she would not, go again through the tearing agony that lay just behind her.

She must, she told herself, be fair. In all their married life she had had no slightest cause to suspect her husband of any infidelity, of any serious flirtation even. If—and she doubted it—he had had his hours of outside erratic conduct, they were unknown to her. Why begin now to assume them? And on nothing more concrete than an idea that had leapt into her mind because he had told her that he had invited a friend, a friend of hers, to a party in his own house. And at a time when she had been, it was likely, more asleep than awake. How could she without anything done or said, or left undone or unsaid, so easily believe him guilty? How be so ready to renounce all confidence in the worth of their life together?

And if, perchance, there were some small something—well, what could it mean? Nothing. There were the boys. There was John Bellew. The thought of these three gave her some slight relief. But she did not look the future in the face. She wanted to feel nothing, to think nothing; simply to believe that it was all silly invention on her part. Yet she could not. Not quite.

Christmas, with its unreality, its hectic rush, its false gaiety, came and went. Irene was thankful for the confused unrest of the season. Its irksomeness, its crowds, its inane and insincere repetitions of genialities, pushed between her and the contemplation of her growing unhappiness.

She was thankful, too, for the continued absence of Clare, who, John Bellew having returned from a long stay in Canada, had withdrawn to that other life of hers, remote and inaccessible. But beating against the walled prison of Irene's thoughts was the shunned fancy that, though absent, Clare Kendry was still present, that she was close.

Brian, too, had withdrawn. The house contained his outward self and his belongings. He came and went with his usual noiseless irregularity. He sat across from her at table. He slept in his room next to hers at night. But he was remote and inaccessible. No use pretending that he was happy, that things were the same as they had always been. He wasn't and they weren't. However, she assured herself, it needn't necessarily be because of anything that involved Clare. It was, it must be, another manifestation of the old longing.

But she did wish it were spring, March, so that Clare would be sailing, out of her life and Brian's. Though she had come almost to believe that there was nothing but generous friendship between those two, she was very tired of Clare Kendry.

She wanted to be free of her, and of her furtive comings and goings. If something would only happen, something that would make John Bellew decide on an earlier departure, or that would remove Clare. Anything. She didn't care what. Not even if it were that Clare's Margery were ill, or dying. Not even if Bellew should discover—

She drew a quick, sharp breath. And for a long time sat staring down at the hands in her lap. Strange, she had not before realized how easily she could put Clare out of her life! She had only to tell John Bellew that his wife—No. Not that! But if he should somehow learn of these Harlem visits— Why should she hesitate? Why spare Clare?

But she shrank away from the idea of telling that man, Clare Kendry's white husband, anything that would lead him to suspect that his wife was a Negro. Nor could she write it, or telephone it, or tell it to someone else who would tell him.

She was caught between two allegiances, different, yet the same. Herself. Her race. Race! The thing that bound and suffocated her. Whatever steps she took, or if she took none at all, something would be crushed. A person or the race. Clare, herself, or the race. Or, it might be, all three. Nothing, she imagined, was ever more completely sardonic.

Sitting alone in the quiet living-room in the pleasant firelight, Irene Redfield wished, for the first time in her life, that she had not been born a Negro. For the first time she suffered and rebelled because she was unable to disregard the burden of race. It was, she cried silently, enough to suffer as a woman, an individual, on one's own account, without having to suffer for the race as well. It was a brutality, and undeserved. Surely, no other people so cursed as Ham's dark children.[1]

Nevertheless, her weakness, her shrinking, her own inability to compass the thing, did not prevent her from wishing fervently that, in some way with which she had no concern, John Bellew would discover, not that his wife had a touch of the tar-brush—Irene didn't want that—but that she was spending all the time that he was out of the city in black Harlem. Only that. It would be enough to rid her forever of Clare Kendry.

THREE

As if in answer to her wish, the very next day Irene came face to face with Bellew.

She had gone downtown with Felise Freeland to shop. The day was an exceptionally cold one, with a strong wind that had whipped a dusky red into Felise's smooth golden cheeks and driven moisture into Irene's soft brown eyes.

Clinging to each other, with heads bent against the wind, they turned out of the Avenue[1] into Fifty-seventh Street. A sudden bluster flung them around the corner with unexpected quickness and they collided with a man.

"Pardon," Irene begged laughingly, and looked up into the face of Clare Kendry's husband.

"Mrs. Redfield!"

His hat came off. He held out his hand, smiling genially.

But the smile faded at once. Surprise, incredulity, and—was it understanding?—passed over his features.

He had, Irene knew, become conscious of Felise, golden, with curly black Negro hair, whose arm was still linked in her own. She was sure, now, of the understanding in his face, as he looked at her again and then back at Felise. And displeasure.

He didn't, however, withdraw his outstretched hand. Not at once.

But Irene didn't take it. Instinctively, in the first glance of recognition, her face had become a mask. Now she turned on him a totally uncomprehending look, a bit questioning. Seeing that he still stood with hand outstretched, she gave him the cool appraising stare which she reserved for mashers,[2] and drew Felise on.

Felise drawled: "Aha! Been 'passing,' have you? Well, I've queered that."[3]

"Yes, I'm afraid you have."

"Why, Irene Redfield! You sound as if you cared terribly. I'm sorry."

"I do, but not for the reason you think. I don't believe I've ever gone native[4] in my life except for the sake of convenience, restaurants, theatre tickets, and things like that. Never socially I mean, except once. You've just passed the only person that I've ever met disguised as a white woman."

"Awfully sorry. Be sure your sin will find you out and all that. Tell me about it."

"I'd like to. It would amuse you. But I can't."

Felise's laughter was as languidly nonchalant as her cool voice. "Can it be possible that the honest Irene has— Oh, do look at that coat! There. The red one. Isn't it a dream?"

Irene was thinking: "I had my chance and didn't take it. I had only to speak and to introduce him to Felise with the casual remark that he was Clare's husband. Only that. Fool. Fool." That instinctive loyalty to a race. Why couldn't she get free of it? Why should it include Clare? Clare, who'd shown little enough consideration for her, and hers. What she felt was not so much resentment as a dull despair because she could not change herself in this respect, could not separate individuals from the race, herself from Clare Kendry.

"Let's go home, Felise. I'm so tired I could drop."

"Why, we haven't done half the things we planned."

"I know, but it's too cold to be running all over town. But you stay down if you want to."

"I think I'll do that, if you don't mind."

And now another problem confronted Irene. She must tell Clare of this meeting. Warn her. But how? She hadn't seen her for days. Writing and telephoning were equally unsafe. And even if it was possible to get in touch with her, what good would it do? If Bellew hadn't concluded that he'd made a mistake, if he was certain of her identity—and he was nobody's fool—telling Clare wouldn't avert the results of the encounter.

Besides, it was too late. Whatever was in store for Clare Kendry had already overtaken her.

Irene was conscious of a feeling of relieved thankfulness at the thought that she was probably rid of Clare, and without having lifted a finger or uttered one word.

But she did mean to tell Brian about meeting John Bellew.

But that, it seemed, was impossible. Strange. Something held her back. Each time she was on the verge of saying: "I ran into Clare's husband on the street downtown today. I'm sure he recognized me, and Felise was with me," she failed to speak. It sounded too much like the warning she wanted it to be. Not even in the presence of the boys at dinner could she make the bare statement.

The evening dragged. At last she said good-night and went upstairs, the words unsaid.

She thought: "Why didn't I tell him? Why didn't I? If trouble comes from this, I'll never forgive myself. I'll tell him when he comes up."

She took up a book, but she could not read, so oppressed was she by a nameless foreboding.

What if Bellew should divorce Clare? Could he? There was the Rhinelander case.[5] But in France, in Paris, such things were very easy. If he divorced her—If Clare were free—But of all the things that could happen, that was the one she did not want. She must get her mind away from that possibility. She must.

Then came a thought which she tried to drive away. If Clare should die! Then—Oh, it was vile! To think, yes, to wish that! She felt faint and sick. But the thought stayed with her. She could not get rid of it.

She heard the outer door open. Close. Brian had gone out. She turned her face into her pillow to cry. But no tears came.

She lay there awake, thinking of things past. Of her courtship and marriage and Junior's birth. Of the time they had bought the house in which they had lived so long and so happily. Of the time Ted had passed his pneumonia crisis and they knew he would live. And of other sweet painful memories that would never come again.

Above everything else she had wanted, had striven, to keep undisturbed the pleasant routine of her life. And now Clare Kendry had come into it, and with her the menace of imper-manence.

"Dear God," she prayed, "make March come quickly."

By and by she slept.

FOUR

The next morning brought with it a snowstorm that lasted throughout the day.

After a breakfast, which had been eaten almost in silence and which she was relieved to have done with, Irene Redfield lingered for a little while in the downstairs hall, looking out at the soft flakes fluttering down. She was watching them immediately fill some ugly irregular gaps left by the feet of hurrying pedestrians when Zulena came to her, saying: "The telephone, Mrs. Redfield. It's Mrs. Bellew."

"Take the message, Zulena, please."

Though she continued to stare out of the window, Irene saw nothing now, stabbed as she was by fear—and hope. Had anything happened between Clare and Bellew? And if so, what? And was she to be freed at last from the aching anxiety of the past weeks? Or was there to be more, and worse? She had a wrestling moment, in which it seemed that she must rush after Zulena and hear for herself what it was that Clare had to say. But she waited.

Zulena, when she came back, said: "She says, ma'am, that she'll be able to go to Mrs. Freeland's tonight. She'll be here some time between eight and nine."

"Thank you, Zulena."

The day dragged on to its end.

At dinner Brian spoke bitterly of a lynching that he had been reading about in the evening paper.

"Dad, why is it that they only lynch coloured people?" Ted asked.

"Because they hate 'em, son."

"Brian!" Irene's voice was a plea and a rebuke.

Ted said: "Oh! And why do they hate 'em?"

"Because they are afraid of them."

"But what makes them afraid of 'em?"

"Because—"

"Brian!"

"It seems, son, that is a subject we can't go into at the moment without distressing the ladies of our family," he told the boy with mock seriousness, "but we'll take it up some time when we're alone together."

Ted nodded in his engaging grave way. "I see. Maybe we can talk about it tomorrow on the way to school."

"That'll be fine."

"Brian!"

"Mother," Junior remarked, "that's the third time you've said 'Brian' like that."

"But not the last, Junior, never you fear," his father told him.

After the boys had gone up to their own floor, Irene said suavely: "I do wish, Brian, that you wouldn't talk about lynching before Ted and Junior. It was really inexcusable for you to bring up a thing like that at dinner. There'll be time enough for them to learn about such horrible things when they're older."

"You're absolutely wrong! If, as you're so determined, they've got to live in this damned country, they'd better find out what sort of thing they're up against as soon as possible. The earlier they learn it, the better prepared they'll be."

"I don't agree. I want their childhood to be happy and as free from the knowledge of such things as it possibly can be."

"Very laudable," was Brian's sarcastic answer. "Very laudable indeed, all things considered. But can it?"

"Certainly it can. If you'll only do your part."

"Stuff! You know as well as I do, Irene, that it can't. What was the use of our trying to keep them from learning the word 'nigger' and its connotation? They found out, didn't they? And how? Because somebody called Junior a dirty nigger."

"Just the same you're not to talk to them about the race problem. I won't have it."

They glared at each other.

"I tell you, Irene, they've got to know these things, and it might as well be now as later."

"They do not!" she insisted, forcing back the tears of anger that were threatening to fall.

Brian growled: "I can't understand how anybody as intelligent as you like to think you are can show evidences of such stupidity." He looked at her in a puzzled harassed way.

"Stupid!" she cried. "Is it stupid to want my children to be happy?" Her lips were quivering.

"At the expense of proper preparation for life and their future happiness, yes. And I'd feel I hadn't done my duty by them if I didn't give them some inkling of what's before them. It's the least I can do. I wanted to get them out of this hellish place years ago. You wouldn't let me. I gave up the idea, because you objected. Don't expect me to give up everything."

Under the lash of his words she was silent. Before any answer came to her, he had turned and gone from the room.

Sitting there alone in the forsaken dining-room, unconsciously pressing the hands lying in her lap, tightly together, she was seized by a convulsion of shivering. For, to her, there had been something ominous in the scene that she had just had with her husband. Over and over in her mind his last words: "Don't expect me to give up everything," repeated themselves. What had they meant? What could they mean? Clare Kendry?

Surely, she was going mad with fear and suspicion. She must not work herself up. She must not! Where were all the self-control, the common sense, that she was so proud of? Now, if ever, was the time for it.

Clare would soon be there. She must hurry or she would be late again, and those two would wait for her downstairs together, as they had done so often since that first time, which now seemed so long ago. Had it been really only last October? Why, she felt years, not months, older.

Drearily she rose from her chair and went upstairs to set about the business of dressing to go out when she would far rather have remained at home. During the process she wondered, for the hundredth time, why she hadn't told Brian about herself and Felise running into Bellew the day before, and for the hundredth time she turned away from acknowledging to herself the real reason for keeping back the information.

When Clare arrived, radiant in a shining red gown, Irene had not finished dressing. But her smile scarcely hesitated as she greeted her, saying: "I always seem to keep C. P. time,[1] don't I? We hardly expected you to be able to come. Felise will be pleased. How nice you look."

Clare kissed a bare shoulder, seeming not to notice a slight shrinking.

"I hadn't an idea in the world, myself, that I'd be able to make it; but Jack had to run down to Philadelphia unexpectedly. So here I am."

Irene looked up, a flood of speech on her lips. "Philadelphia. That's not very far, is it? Clare, I—?"

She stopped, one of her hands clutching the side of her stool, the other lying clenched on the dressing-table. Why didn't she go on and tell Clare about meeting Bellew? Why couldn't she?

But Clare didn't notice the unfinished sentence. She laughed and said lightly: "It's far enough for me. Anywhere, away from me, is far enough. I'm not particular."

Irene passed a hand over her eyes to shut out the accusing face in the glass before her. With one corner of her mind she wondered how long she had looked like that, drawn and haggard and—yes, frightened. Or was it only imagination?

"Clare," she asked, "have you ever seriously thought what it would mean if he should find you out?"

"Yes."

"Oh! You have! And what you'd do in that case?"

"Yes." And having said it, Clare Kendry smiled quickly, a smile that came and went like a flash, leaving untouched the gravity of her face.

That smile and the quiet resolution of that one word, "yes,"

filled Irene with a primitive paralysing dread. Her hands were
numb, her feet like ice, her heart like a stone weight. Even her
tongue was like a heavy dying thing. There were long spaces
between the words as she asked: "And what should you do?"

Clare, who was sunk in a deep chair, her eyes far away,
seemed wrapped in some pleasant impenetrable reflection. To
Irene, sitting expectantly upright, it was an interminable time
before she dragged herself back to the present to say calmly:
"I'd do what I want to do more than anything else right now.
I'd come up here to live. Harlem, I mean. Then I'd be able to
do as I please, when I please."

Irene leaned forward, cold and tense. "And what about Margery?" Her voice was a strained whisper.

"Margery?" Clare repeated, letting her eyes flutter over
Irene's concerned face. "Just this, 'Rene. If it wasn't for her,
I'd do it anyway. She's all that holds me back. But if Jack finds
out, if our marriage is broken, that lets me out. Doesn't it?"

Her gentle resigned tone, her air of innocent candour, appeared, to her listener, spurious. A conviction that the words
were intended as a warning took possession of Irene. She remembered that Clare Kendry had always seemed to know what
other people were thinking. Her compressed lips grew firm
and obdurate. Well, she wouldn't know this time.

She said: "Do go downstairs and talk to Brian. He's got a
mad on."

Though she had determined that Clare should not get at her
thoughts and fears, the words had sprung, unthought of, to
her lips. It was as if they had come from some outer layer of
callousness that had no relation to her tortured heart. And
they had been, she realized, precisely the right words for her
purpose.

For as Clare got up and went out, she saw that that arrange-
ment was as good as her first plan of keeping her waiting up
there while she dressed—or better. She would only have hin-
dered and rasped her. And what matter if those two spent one
hour, more or less, alone together, one or many, now that everything had happened between them?

Ah! The first time that she had allowed herself to admit to herself that everything had happened, had not forced herself to believe, to hope, that nothing irrevocable had been consummated! Well, it had happened. She knew it, and knew that she knew it.

She was surprised that, having thought the thought, conceded the fact, she was no more hurt, cared no more, than during her previous frenzied endeavours to escape it. And this absence of acute, unbearable pain seemed to her unjust, as if she had been denied some exquisite solace of suffering which the full acknowledgment should have given her.

Was it, perhaps, that she had endured all that a woman could endure of tormenting humiliation and fear? Or was it that she lacked the capacity for the acme of suffering? "No, no!" she denied fiercely. "I'm human like everybody else. It's just that I'm so tired, so worn out, I can't feel any more." But she did not really believe that.

Security. Was it just a word? If not, then was it only by the sacrifice of other things, happiness, love, or some wild ecstasy that she had never known, that it could be obtained? And did too much striving, too much faith in safety and permanence, unfit one for these other things?

Irene didn't know, couldn't decide, though for a long time she sat questioning and trying to understand. Yet all the while, in spite of her searchings and feeling of frustration, she was aware that, to her, security was the most important and desired thing in life. Not for any of the others, or for all of them, would she exchange it. She wanted only to be tranquil. Only, unmolested, to be allowed to direct for their own best good the lives of her sons and her husband.

Now that she had relieved herself of what was almost like a guilty knowledge, admitted that which by some sixth sense she had long known, she could again reach out for plans. Could think again of ways to keep Brian by her side, and in New York. For she would not go to Brazil. She belonged in this land of rising towers. She was an American. She grew from this soil, and she would not be uprooted. Not even because of Clare Kendry, or a hundred Clare Kendrys.

Brian, too, belonged here. His duty was to her and to his boys.

Strange, that she couldn't now be sure that she had ever truly known love. Not even for Brian. He was her husband and the father of her sons. But was he anything more? Had she ever wanted or tried for more? In that hour she thought not.

Nevertheless, she meant to keep him. Her freshly painted lips narrowed to a thin straight line. True, she had left off trying to believe that he and Clare loved and yet did not love, but she still intended to hold fast to the outer shell of her marriage, to keep her life fixed, certain. Brought to the edge of distasteful reality, her fastidious nature did not recoil. Better, far better, to share him than to lose him completely. Oh, she could close her eyes, if need be. She could bear it. She could bear anything. And there was March ahead. March and the departure of Clare.

Horribly clear, she could now see the reason for her instinct to withhold—omit, rather—her news of the encounter with Bellew. If Clare was freed, anything might happen.

She paused in her dressing, seeing with perfect clearness that dark truth which she had from that first October afternoon felt about Clare Kendry and of which Clare herself had once warned her—that she got the things she wanted because she met the great condition of conquest, sacrifice. If she wanted Brian, Clare wouldn't revolt from the lack of money or place. It was as she had said, only Margery kept her from throwing all that away. And if things were taken out of her hands— Even if she was only alarmed, only suspected that such a thing was about to occur, anything might happen. Anything.

No! At all costs, Clare was not to know of that meeting with Bellew. Nor was Brian. It would only weaken her own power to keep him.

They would never know from her that he was on his way to suspecting the truth about his wife. And she would do anything, risk anything, to prevent him from finding out that truth. How fortunate that she had obeyed her instinct and omitted to recognize Bellew!

———

"Ever go up to the sixth floor, Clare?" Brian asked as he stopped the car and got out to open the door for them.

"Why, of course! We're on the seventeenth."

"I mean, did you ever go up by nigger-power?"[2]

"That's good!" Clare laughed. "Ask 'Rene. My father was a janitor, you know, in the good old days before every ramshackle flat had its elevator. But you can't mean we've got to walk up? Not here!"

"Yes, here. And Felise lives at the very top," Irene told her.

"What on earth for?"

"I believe she claims it discourages the casual visitor."

"And she's probably right. Hard on herself, though."

Brian said: "Yes, a bit. But she says she'd rather be dead than bored."

"Oh, a garden! And how lovely with that undisturbed snow!"

"Yes, isn't it? But keep to the walk with those foolish thin shoes. You too, Irene."

Irene walked beside them on the cleared cement path that split the whiteness of the courtyard garden. She felt a something in the air, something that had been between those two and would be again. It was like a live thing pressing against her. In a quick furtive glance she saw Clare clinging to Brian's other arm. She was looking at him with that provocative upward glance of hers, and his eyes were fastened on her face with what seemed to Irene an expression of wistful eagerness.

"It's this entrance, I believe," she informed them in quite her ordinary voice.

"Mind," Brian told Clare, "you don't fall by the wayside before the fourth floor. They absolutely refuse to carry anyone up more than the last two flights."

"Don't be silly!" Irene snapped.

The party began gaily.

Dave Freeland was at his best, brilliant, crystal clear, and sparkling. Felise, too, was amusing, and not so sarcastic as usual, because she liked the dozen or so guests that dotted the long, untidy living-room. Brian was witty, though, Irene noted, his remarks were somewhat more barbed than was customary even with him. And there was Ralph Hazelton, throwing non-sensical shining things into the pool of talk, which the others, even Clare, picked up and flung back with fresh adornment.

Only Irene wasn't merry. She sat almost silent, smiling now and then, that she might appear amused.

"What's the matter, Irene?" someone asked. "Taken a vow never to laugh, or something? You're as sober as a judge."

"No. It's simply that the rest of you are so clever that I'm speechless, absolutely stunned."

"No wonder," Dave Freeland remarked, "that you're on the verge of tears. You haven't a drink. What'll you take?"

"Thanks. If I must take something, make it a glass of ginger-ale and three drops of Scotch. The Scotch first, please. Then the ice, then the ginger ale."

"Heavens! Don't attempt to mix that yourself, Dave darling. Have the butler in," Felise mocked.

"Yes, do. And the footman." Irene laughed a little, then said: "It seems dreadfully warm in here. Mind if I open this window?" With that she pushed open one of the long casement-windows of which the Freelands were so proud.

It had stopped snowing some two or three hours back. The moon was just rising, and far behind the tall buildings a few stars were creeping out. Irene finished her cigarette and threw it out, watching the tiny spark drop slowly down to the white ground below.

Someone in the room had turned on the phonograph. Or was it the radio? She didn't know which she disliked more. And nobody was listening to its blare. The talking, the laugh-ter never for a minute ceased. Why must they have more noise?

Dave came with her drink. "You ought not," he told her, "to stand there like that. You'll take cold. Come along and talk to me, or listen to me gabble." Taking her arm, he led her across the room. They had just found seats when the door-bell rang and Felise called over to him to go and answer it.

In the next moment Irene heard his voice in the hall, carelessly polite: "Your wife? Sorry. I'm afraid you're wrong. Perhaps next—"

Then the roar of John Bellew's voice above all the other noises of the room: "I'm *not* wrong! I've been to the Redfields and I know she's with them. You'd better stand out of my way and save yourself trouble in the end."

"What is it, Dave?" Felise ran out to the door.

And so did Brian. Irene heard him saying: "I'm Redfield. What the devil's the matter with you?"

But Bellew didn't heed him. He pushed past them all into the room and strode towards Clare. They all looked at her as she got up from her chair, backing a little from his approach.

"So you're a nigger, a damned dirty nigger!" His voice was a snarl and a moan, an expression of rage and of pain.

Everything was in confusion. The men had sprung forward. Felise had leapt between them and Bellew. She said quickly: "Careful. You're the only white man here." And the silver chill of her voice, as well as her words, was a warning.

Clare stood at the window, as composed as if everyone were not staring at her in curiosity and wonder, as if the whole structure of her life were not lying in fragments before her. She seemed unaware of any danger or uncaring. There was even a faint smile on her full, red lips, and in her shining eyes.

It was that smile that maddened Irene. She ran across the room, her terror tinged with ferocity, and laid a hand on Clare's bare arm. One thought possessed her. She couldn't have Clare Kendry cast aside by Bellew. She couldn't have her free.

Before them stood John Bellew, speechless now in his hurt and anger. Beyond them the little huddle of other people, and Brian stepping out from among them.

What happened next, Irene Redfield never afterwards allowed herself to remember. Never clearly.

One moment Clare had been there, a vital glowing thing, like a flame of red and gold. The next she was gone.

There was a gasp of horror, and above it a sound not quite human, like a beast in agony. "Nig! My God! Nig!"

A frenzied rush of feet down long flights of stairs. The slamming of distant doors. Voices.

Irene stayed behind. She sat down and remained quite still, staring at a ridiculous Japanese print on the wall across the room.

Gone! The soft white face, the bright hair, the disturbing scarlet mouth, the dreaming eyes, the caressing smile, the whole torturing loveliness that had been Clare Kendry. That beauty that had torn at Irene's placid life. Gone! The mocking daring, the gallantry of her pose, the ringing bells of her laughter.

Irene wasn't sorry. She was amazed, incredulous almost.

What would the others think? That Clare had fallen? That she had deliberately leaned backward? Certainly one or the other. Not—

But she mustn't, she warned herself, think of that. She was too tired, and too shocked. And, indeed, both were true. She was utterly weary, and she was violently staggered. But her thoughts reeled on. If only she could be as free of mental as she was of bodily vigour; could only put from her memory the vision of her hand on Clare's arm!

"It was an accident, a terrible accident," she muttered fiercely. "It *was*."

People were coming up the stairs. Through the still open door their steps and talk sounded nearer, nearer.

Quickly she stood up and went noiselessly into the bedroom and closed the door softly behind her.

Her thoughts raced. Ought she to have stayed? Should she go back out there to them? But there would be questions. She hadn't thought of them, of afterwards, of this. She had thought of nothing in that sudden moment of action.

It was cold. Icy chills ran up her spine and over her bare neck and shoulders.

In the room outside there were voices. Dave Freeland's and others that she did not recognize.

Should she put on her coat? Felise had rushed down without any wrap. So had all the others. So had Brian. Brian! He mustn't take cold. She took up his coat and left her own. At the door she paused for a moment, listening fearfully. She heard nothing. No voices. No footsteps. Very slowly she opened the door. The room was empty. She went out.

In the hall below she heard dimly the sound of feet going down the steps, of a door being opened and closed, and of voices far away.

Down, down, down, she went, Brian's great coat clutched in her shivering arms and trailing a little on each step behind her.

What was she to say to them when at last she had finished going down those endless stairs? She should have rushed out when they did. What reason could she give for her dallying behind? Even she didn't know why she had done that. And what else would she be asked? There had been her hand reaching out towards Clare. What about that?

In the midst of her wonderings and questionings came a thought so terrifying, so horrible, that she had had to grasp hold of the banister to save herself from pitching downwards. A cold perspiration drenched her shaking body. Her breath came short in sharp and painful gasps.

What if Clare was not dead?

She felt nauseated, as much at the idea of the glorious body mutilated as from fear.

How she managed to make the rest of the journey without fainting she never knew. But at last she was down. Just at the bottom she came on the others, surrounded by a little circle of strangers. They were all speaking in whispers, or in the awed, discreetly lowered tones adapted to the presence of disaster. In the first instant she wanted to turn and rush back up the way she had come. Then a calm desperation came over her. She braced herself, physically and mentally.

"Here's Irene now," Dave Freeland announced, and told her that, having only just missed her, they had concluded that she had fainted or something like that, and were on the way to find out about her. Felise, she saw, was holding on to his arm, all the insolent nonchalance gone out of her, and the golden brown of her handsome face changed to a queer mauve colour.

Irene made no indication that she had heard Freeland, but went straight to Brian. His face looked aged and altered, and his lips were purple and trembling. She had a great longing to comfort him, to charm away his suffering and horror. But she was helpless, having so completely lost control of his mind and heart.

She stammered: "Is she—is she—?"

It was Felise who answered. "Instantly, we think."

Irene struggled against the sob of thankfulness that rose in her throat. Choked down, it turned to a whimper, like a hurt child's. Someone laid a hand on her shoulder in a soothing gesture. Brian wrapped his coat about her. She began to cry rackingly, her entire body heaving with convulsive sobs. He made a slight perfunctory attempt to comfort her.

"There, there, Irene. You mustn't. You'll make yourself sick. She's—" His voice broke suddenly.

As from a long distance she heard Ralph Hazelton's voice saying: "I was looking right at her. She just tumbled over and was gone before you could say 'Jack Robinson.' Fainted, I guess. Lord! It was quick. Quickest thing I ever saw in all my life."

"It's impossible, I tell you! Absolutely impossible!"

It was Brian who spoke in that frenzied hoarse voice, which Irene had never heard before. Her knees quaked under her.

Dave Freeland said: "Just a minute, Brian. Irene was there beside her. Let's hear what she has to say."

She had a moment of stark craven fear. "Oh God," she thought, prayed, "help me."

A strange man, official and authoritative, addressed her. "You're sure she fell? Her husband didn't give her a shove or anything like that, as Dr. Redfield seems to think?"

For the first time she was aware that Bellew was not in the little group shivering in the small hallway. What did that mean? As she began to work it out in her numbed mind, she was shaken with another hideous trembling. Not that! Oh, not that!

"No, no!" she protested. "I'm quite certain that he didn't. I was there, too. As close as he was. She just fell, before anybody could stop her. I—"

Her quaking knees gave way under her. She moaned and

sank down, moaned again. Through the great heaviness that submerged and drowned her she was dimly conscious of strong arms lifting her up. Then everything was dark.

Centuries after, she heard the strange man saying: "Death by misadventure, I'm inclined to believe. Let's go up and have another look at that window."

EXPLANATORY NOTES

DEDICATION

1. *Carl Van Vechten*: (1886–1964), *New York Times* music critic (1906–12), drama critic, novelist, and photographer, a leading white supporter of the 1920s black cultural and literary movement in New York, known for his interracial parties and excursions to Harlem. Controversial during the Harlem Renaissance or New Negro movement because of his novel *Nigger Heaven* (1926), he was Larsen's friend and mentor, instrumental in the publication of her first novel, *Quicksand* (1928).

2. *Fania Marinoff*: (1887–1972), New York stage and film actress, Russian-born wife of Carl Van Vechten, and hostess of interracial gatherings during the Harlem Renaissance.

EPIGRAPH

1. *"One three centuries removed/ . . . /What is Africa to me?"*: Lines from the poem "Heritage," from *Color* (Harper, New York, 1925), a volume of poetry by Countée Cullen. Perhaps his best-known poem, "Heritage" examined the role of culture in the shaping of identity and questioned the dialogic between an African past and an European-influenced present for African-Americans.

2. *Countée Cullen*: (1903–46), one of the celebrated poets of the Harlem Renaissance, known for his lyrical voice and evocation of the British Romantic poet, John Keats (1795–1821). The precocious adopted son of a leading Harlem minister, Rev. Frederick Asbury Cullen (1868–1946), he began publishing poetry

at the age of fifteen. When he graduated Phi Beta Kappa from New York University in 1925, he was widely recognized as a poet whose poems had already appeared in prestigious national magazines and whose first collection of poems, *Color*, was to be published by Harper & Brothers in the year of his college graduation. Throughout the remaining years of the 1920s, Cullen amassed prizes, awards, and an M.A. in English from Harvard University (1926). Although his verse frequently examined issues of racial heritage and identity, he struggled against having his poetry racialized.

PART ONE: ENCOUNTER

CHAPTER TWO

1. *car-tracks*: Rails through city streets for the operation of street-cars or trolleys; the Chicago Surface Lines then comprised the largest street-car system in existence.

2. "*The Drayton*": Fictional hotel, modeled on two fashionable Chicago hotels: the Drake (located on the Gold Coast end of Michigan Avenue and Walton Place at Lakeshore Drive) and the Morrison (located in the Loop at Madison and Clark streets in the 1920s and known for its Terrace Garden Restaurant).

3. *Lincoln Park*: North Side Chicago park area, bounded by North Avenue and Fullerton Avenue, Clark Street and Lakeshore Drive; home of the Lincoln Park Zoo, the Chicago Historical Society, and the Chicago Academy of Science.

4. *Packard limousine*: Luxury, chauffeur-driven automobile perfected by J. W. Packard and W. D. Packard and produced from 1899 to 1958.

5. *the Shelby*: Fictional hotel, modeled on the Sherman, a Chicago hotel and restaurant located at Clark and Randolph streets in the Loop.

6. "*Marshall Field's*": Chicago's premiere department store, founded in 1881 and located at Randolph, Wabash, Washington, and State streets. A pioneer in modern retail merchandis-

ing, and in the 1920s the world's largest retail store, Marshall
Field and Company was world-famous for both customer service and for architectural features: Tiffany Dome, Great Clock
(a Chicago landmark), and atrium fountain.

7. *"Idlewild"*: Black resort in Lake County, Michigan, seventy-
nine miles north of Grand Rapids. Founded in 1912 and developed over the next decade, Idlewild was marketed nationally
to middle-class urbanites as a first-class vacation retreat with
beaches, crystal lake waters, fish and game, wild flowers, hotel
accommodations, and myriad opportunities for outdoor sports.
By the late 1920s, Idlewild was the premiere black resort in the
United States.

8. *a son of their brother's, on the left hand*: The offspring of a
morganatic marriage or similar legal marriage between partners
of unequal rank or status, in which the partner of lower status
and the couple's offspring are excluded from sharing in the estate. Clare's father, Bob Kendry, is thus the son of a black mother
and a white father, whose racial status he cannot inherit.

9. *"sons and daughters of Ham"*: (Genesis 9:20–27), literally, the
Canaanites, the descendants of Ham, one of the three sons of
Noah, saved from God's destruction of a wicked world by
flooding. Ham was punished for mocking his father's drunken-
ness and nakedness. Ham's punishment for disrespecting his
father fell upon his children who were cursed to become the
slaves of his brothers' children; slave holders in the United States
applied this Biblical account to Africans and used it as a justi-
fication for slavery.

10. *"the tar-brush"*: A reference to African ancestry; derived from
the descriptive saying, "Black as tar."

CHAPTER THREE

1. *"Morgan"*: Fictional hotel modeled on the Morrison. See note
2, Part One, Chapter Two.

2. *"Cottage Grove"*: A major north-south street on the South Side
of Chicago.

3. *"Maryland Avenue—used to be Jackson . . . Near Sixty-third
Street"*: Nella Larsen's personal joke; her parents owned a small

South Side Chicago apartment house on Maryland Avenue, whose name had been changed from Jackson at the time of the 1893 World's Columbian Exposition when the area was marketed as McChesney's World's Fair Subdivision; Sixty-third Street was the business and commercial district in this area, known as Woodland and adjacent to the site of the Columbian Exposition, and where the Chicago Surface Lines had a terminal station and the Illinois Central Railway operated the Woodland Park Station.

4. *wartime in France . . . new gaiety of Budapest*: Clare's account of her sojourn in France, Germany, England, and Austria-Hungary during World War I (1914–1918) and its aftermath (1919–1926), when Europe underwent enormous changes and upheavals in its political, social, and economic life, including workers' strikes in the post-war period (such as the week-long May 1926 General Strike in England by the major transport, railway, and mining unions mentioned in the text), and the emergence of Paris in the 1920s as the capital of the fashion industry.

PART TWO:
RE-ENCOUNTER

CHAPTER ONE

1. *The sardony of it*: Mocking bitterness; scornful, cynical humor; Larsen creates a noun form of the adjective "sardonic."

2. *"Seventh Avenue, and Lenox Avenue . . . 'shine' . . . 'sheba?'"*: Primary streets identified with the heart of 1920s Harlem for their subway stops, theatres, cabarets, restaurants, strolling, and parades; "shine" is slang for a black man, derived from the negative notion of shiny black skin; and "sheba" is slang for a black woman, derived from the Biblical Queen of Sheba (I Kings: 10), an Arabian ruler who brought gold, spices, and precious stones to King Solomon.

3. *"Uplifting the brother's no easy job"*: Uplift, an ethic of service

and racial self-help fueled by self-interests and focused on the black masses, permeated black middle-class ideology from emancipation through the first decades of the twentieth century, when social advancement was considered the distinguishing feature of racial progress. The work of racial uplift for middle-class blacks in the helping professions, such as medicine, teaching, and social work, became more difficult after World War I when mass black migration from the rural South to northern urban areas, in particular New York City and Chicago, threatened to overwhelm the resources for improving the living conditions of poor blacks.

CHAPTER TWO

1. *"Mr. Wentworth"*: Hugh and Bianca Wentworth are characters modeled on novelist Carl Van Vechten and his actress wife, Fania Marinoff, who ignored the social separation of the races in New York by inviting blacks to their home and by frequenting both the public gatherings and the private homes of blacks in the 1920s.

2. *"The Negro Welfare League"*: Fictitious organization based on the National Urban League, established in New York City in 1911 to assist blacks who migrated from rural areas to urban centers in obtaining jobs, housing, education, and services. The National Urban League's official magazine, *Opportunity*, founded in 1923 and edited by sociologist Charles S. Johnson, became one of the major publishing outlets for writers during the Harlem Renaissance.

3. *"to get material to turn into shekels"*: The opportunistic practice of whites from downtown capitalizing on the 1920s' vogue for "things Negro" by spending time uptown in Harlem to collect materials on black culture and race matters—music, dance, styles, beliefs, practices, and trends—to use in their art for profit. Larsen's friend, Carl Van Vechten, was accused of this practice when his 1926 novel, *Nigger Heaven*, appeared to exploit his black acquaintances and the access to Harlem life they had provided him.

CHAPTER THREE

1. "*'butter and egg' men*": Expression for wealthy men or big spenders.
2. "*tripped the light fantastic*": Slang for dancing.
3. "*Dorothy Thompkins*": Fictitious character, probably based on Dorothy Fields (1905–74), a white songwriter who began her career in the 1920s by writing material for black shows at the Cotton Club, and who achieved her first major success by writing songs for the hit show *Blackbirds of 1928*.
4. "*dicty*": High-toned; person assuming airs and mannerisms of the upper class.
5. "*'fay'*": Short form of "ofay," slang for white people.
6. "*Slippin' me, Irene?*": Slang for tricking or hoodwinking, putting something over on someone.

PART THREE: FINALE

CHAPTER ONE

1. "*Eighteenth-century France . . . or the old South*": Places and times placing a high premium on female beauty, in which women might get by being what Larsen terms "intelligent in a purely feminine way."
2. "*Haiti*": Work of art produced in Haiti; Haitian art, in particular painting and sculpture, became popular during the cultural awakening of the Harlem Renaissance for its expressive relation to traditional African forms and to colorful, symbolic representations of black folk life.
3. "*Josephine Baker*": (1906–75), singer, dancer, and entertainer, initially made her mark as "the comedy chorus girl" in *Chocolate Dandies* (1924), after using her comic talents in a Boston production of *Shuffle Along*. In 1925 she was selected for *Revue Negre*, a show headed for Paris; there Baker immediately became a star and a headliner at the Folies Bergère and French nightclubs. By the end of the 1920s, she was the toast of France and the most famous American entertainer in Europe.

4. "Shuffle Along": 1921 musical comedy written by the vaudeville team of Aubrey Lyles (1882–1932) and Flournoy Miller
(1889–1971), with music by Noble Sissle (1889–1975) and Eubie
Blake (1883–1983), and hailed as the first popular all-black
show of the decade and sometimes credited as the opening act
of the Harlem Renaissance.

5. "*Ethel Waters*": (1896–1977), singer, recording artist, and stage
and film actress, was one of the busiest and most popular per-
formers during the 1920s. While still a teenager, she toured in
vaudeville and tent shows as "Sweet Mama Stringbean," but
she graduated to appearances in New York and recordings for
Black Swan records in 1921. She enjoyed success in musical
reviews at New York's Lafayette Theatre (*Tan Town Topics*,
1925; *Too Bad*, 1925; and *Black Bottom Revue*, 1926), and on
Broadway (*Africana*, 1927). Her stardom continued to rise in
Europe and New York during the 1930s, when she also began
working as a dramatic actress.

6. *Dave Freeland*: Character based on the novelist and short story
writer Rudolph Fisher (1897–1934), who was known for his
sharp wit and sparkling conversation. A medical doctor spe-
cializing in roentgenology, Fisher divided his time between his
practice in X-ray technology and his literary career. His satiric
first novel, *The Walls of Jericho*, appeared in 1928 (the same
year as Larsen's *Quicksand*), and contained Fisher's "Introduction to Contemporary Harlemese: Expurgated and Abridged,"
a dictionary of black slang and popular terms used in the 1920s.

CHAPTER TWO

1. *Ham's dark children*: (Genesis 10: 6–20), in the Biblical Table
of Nations, the descendants of Noah's son Ham are the Semitic-
speaking people of Canaan, then belonging to Egypt, and the
Hamitic-speaking people of Northern Africa, including Egypt,
Ethiopia, and Nubia.

CHAPTER THREE

1. *the Avenue*: Fifth Avenue, the area of New York City known
for fine shopping and exclusive stores.

2. *mashers*: Men making unwelcome sexual advances or passes.
3. *"queered"*: Slang for thwart, spoil, reverse, or ruin.
4. *"gone native"*: Term for passing.
5. *the Rhinelander case*: A highly publicized 1920s trial involving race, sex, marriage, and passing. Leonard Kip Rhinelander, a member of one of New York's wealthiest and oldest families, married a mulatto chamber maid, Alice B. Jones, on 14 October 1924, one week after he had received a share of his family's stocks, real estate, jewels, and cash. After a month of marriage and under pressure from his family, Rhinelander sought an annulment on the grounds that Alice had fraudulently concealed her race. The sensational trial was front-page news in the New York newspapers for over one year, during which time Alice Jones Rhinelander was required to disrobe on the witness stand for an examination of her skin, frank courtship letters were read into evidence, and Leonard Rhinelander contradicted himself about his knowledge of Alice's race. The New York State Supreme Court jury found on April 5, 1925 that Alice had not been fraudulent about her racial identity and no annulment was granted. Leonard Rhinelander appealed the decision and fought it through the legal system for another year, but lost his appeals. In 1927, Alice Jones Rhinelander filed a suit for separation from her husband, whom she charged with abandonment, and in 1929, she sued his father, Philip Rhinelander, for ruining her marriage. When the case finally ended in 1929, Alice Jones received $31,500, plus $3,600 payable quarterly for the rest of her life; the divorce decree provided that she could no longer use the Rhinelander name. Kip Rhinelander died four years later of pneumonia.

CHAPTER FOUR

1. *"C. P. time"*: Colored People's time, euphemism for being late.
2. *"nigger-power"*: Reference to having to expend physical effort, sweat, and hard work in order to achieve something.